WORLD SERIES

WORLD SERIES

John R. Tunis

GULLIVER BOOKS

HARCOURT BRACE JOVANOVICH, PUBLISHERS

San Diego   New York   London

To Luke Sewell,
who says I ask more questions
than anyone in the United States
except Bob Feller.

HBJ

Text copyright © 1941 by Lucy R. Tunis
Copyright renewed 1969 by Lucy R. Tunis
Introduction copyright © 1987 by Harcourt Brace Jovanovich, Inc.

Library of Congress Cataloging-in-Publication Data
Tunis, John Roberts, 1889–
    World series.
    "Gulliver books."
    Reprint. Originally published: New York: Harcourt Brace, 1941.
    Summary: Roy Tucker, the Kid from Tomkinsville, joins the rest
of his Dodger teammates in a come-from-behind battle for the series
title.
    [1. Baseball — Fiction] I. Title.
PZ7.T8236Wo 1987   [Fic]   86-27014
ISBN 0-15-200651-6

Designed by Francesca Smith
Frontispiece by Paul Bacon
Printed in the United States of America
    B C D E

Introduction

In writing this book, John R. Tunis took a tip from every baseball player who has ever taken the field in the Fall Classic: The World Series is a lifetime unto itself, a separate existence in which every detail demands scrutiny, every action becomes crucial. They've *all* said this, from Babe Ruth to George Brett. Nothing short of *greatness* is at stake—a kind of immortality can be won or lost, all within seven supremely special games. It's wonderful, and it's scary. No fan or player ever fails to feel, on the eve of the first Series game, that something historic is about to unfold, and that some grand secret is about to be revealed in a complex marvel of sport at its best.

To fully give us the density and magic of the Series, Tunis shifts gears from the usual pace of writing that dramatizes a season or two in one book. Here he, too, stops the world for the Series, creates a new intensity of focus, lavishes a fascinated attention on each nuance of action, expectation, and decision. The result: a thrilling new kind of reading experience.

What Tunis does, really, is rob us of the luxury of patience. No longer can we read with the assurance that the leisurely development of plot will make everything all right in due course, turning perils into stepping-stones on the long path to success. There are no more stepping-stones: We have arrived at the end of the path on Page One. Any wrongs threaten to stay wrong, now; there simply isn't time for the course of nature to right them. If a player is injured in Chapter 3, we can't turn the page with a knowing smile, assured that he'll heal by Chapter 18, when he's really needed. He's needed *now*. And suddenly, for a moment, the bottom falls out for us: "Wait," we say, "things are happening too fast. . . ."

But of course there's no stopping Tunis, or the Series, or the burning will of the powerful Cleveland team determined to spoil the heroic Dodgers' season chronicled in *The Kid from Tomkinsville*. That season, like that book, is over. And although we are picking up the same characters only a week after that novel's last page, the thrill of Roy Tucker's stardom—and the Dodgers' pennant—is history. *World Series* is a very unusual sequel: It takes everything we gained from the long, marvelous struggle to the top in *The Kid from Tomkinsville*, and puts it all on the line. Double or nothing, seven cards, face down.

Of course, we do have good company in our suspense.

Roy is here, and Razzle, and Fat Stuff and Dave Leonard and Mr. MacManus . . . even old Chiselbeak and Stubblebeard. The colorful, intriguing Dodgers quickly capture allegiance of the readers who met them in *The Kid from Tomkinsville* and the new readers who haven't met them before. But when Cleveland goes up three games to one, we may ask if we really *want* to be so bound up in the fate of these guys from Brooklyn. It's too late to step coolly back, though — Tunis has us right where he wants us: Each reader is a part of this team by now, and we must rally our spirit along with them.

Rally. That's what we need. Hey, there's two out, but look — Harry Street's drawn a walk, and it looks like Dave himself is going to pinch hit for Fat Stuff. . . .

It looks like we are going to stick in the grip of this great tale, too, until the last pitch has been thrown, the last whistling line drive has been caught, the last tense sentence has reached its period. When it's over, all of a sudden we'll want to take back the urgent haste with which we raced toward the end of our suspense — we'll want to have it all over again, every hit, every out, every break, good or bad. We'll want these seven games — this separate lifetime — forever.

And we'll *have* it forever, thanks to Tunis. Because a great book, like a great World Series, stays in front of us, in all its detail and completeness. Its secrets are never wholly revealed, and the thrill of seeking them is never over.

— Bruce Brooks

1

This was different.

It was the same room, same scene, same faces. Yet terribly different, too. In the corner were the black equipment trunks with BROOKLYN BASEBALL CLUB painted in red on the sides. There were the bats slung on top of the green lockers, the clean shirts with their big numbers in blue hanging from wire hangers inside. As usual, Dave Leonard was sitting with his arms folded over the back of a chair, his toothpick doing its dance across his mouth while he looked around. At Karl Case spitting into his glove, at Harry Street nervously chewing, at Ed Davis, his chin in his hands, gazing solemnly ahead. At Hank West who had just learned he was going to catch. As usual, Chiselbeak, the locker man, wound through the group taking money and watches for the valuables trunk. In short, the same scene that took place before every game.

Yet this was different. There was a different atmosphere in the room. No one was reading Casey's column in the *Mail*. For once Raz Nugent had stopped talking. Babe Stansworth had tossed away his crossword puzzle, and even Elmer McCaffrey, always late, had his shoes tied and was ready. As a rule they met before the game in the early afternoon. Now it was ten-thirty, and there was a small fire in the stove in the center of the room because the fall morning was brisk and snappy.

Why wouldn't this be different? After all, two — maybe four — thousand dollars were at stake for every man. Four thousand! Imagine what that would do on the farm. Gosh, wouldn't Grandma be tickled if . . .

"Now, boys . . . " Silence over the room as they watched him remove the toothpick from his mouth. "This ball game can be won right here, so better listen carefully." He paused. No one needed that. There was a deep furrow over Red

Allen's face and a frown of concentration on Fat Stuff's usually jovial brow, and Harry Street kept yanking off his cap and running his hand through his hair. Because this was different. No use fooling, this was different. Two . . . maybe four thousand . . .

"Just want you boys to play like you've played for me all season—heads-up, hustling ball. Go into 'em. Upset 'em. Shove 'em hard. Want you should watch 'em careful-like in batting practice, you pitchers; you may be able to tell their weaknesses. This Cleveland club has a star pitcher; they're a smart team all right; they take extra bases every chance they get and never let up. That's why they won the pennant. They play ball like you've played ball all season, which means they're no better than we are. And they're older. 'Cept for Miller and McClusky in center and that kid there at third—what'shisname, Painter—they're an old team. Why . . . that gang is so old they remind me of the Nine Old Men. Don't forget it.

"Remember one thing. If we can stop Hammerstein and Gardiner and McClusky, we've stopped their hitters. We knew Bruce Gordon, Fat Stuff and I did, when we was with the White Sox in nineteen and thirty-four. A high, fast-ball hitter. Center and left, play toward left. You Tucker, I want you should hug that right field line, especially with a man on first. Get that? Jake, when you pitch, keep your fast ball low on Gardiner. Or, in a pinch, I'd throw him a curve. Short and third, play him straightaway. If they're ahead, he'll bunt . . . every time he's lead off man.

"Now this boy McClusky, in center. Yes, he's fast all right. Fields ground balls well. Meets 'em fast and throws quick; don't want to see any of you take extra bases on him unless you're dead sure. . . ."

Gosh! Just think of it. Two . . . maybe four thousand bucks at stake. Four thousand dollars! And a sellout for the first three games, so the papers said. How many was it . . . seventy . . . eighty thousand that Stadium in Cleveland held? Why now, if it was four thousand . . .

"You gettin' all this, Roy? Remember, it's just as important where fielders play as where they are pitched to." Everyone turned toward him. He nodded, although he hadn't heard the last words and Dave knew he hadn't. Dave missed very little.

"Did I understand you McClusky is their only good thrower in the field?" Some managers would have bawled him out; not Dave. That was why Dave could work them harder, get more out of tired men, ask them for more. He always saved things of that sort for private conversation.

"Yep. If you get a chance on the others, why go ahead."

"What about Hammy?" piped up Ed Davis from the rear of the room.

The toothpick went back in Dave's mouth. He glanced at the piece of paper folded in his hand. "I'm coming to him. Hammerstein led the American League in homers this year. We had a scout watching every ball he hit. Here's the report." Dave unfolded another bit of paper as the pitchers leaned forward nervously. "He hit homers on . . . on twenty-two fast balls above the waist and on fourteen curve balls below the waist. The others on curves, high. You can slow up to him any time you want to."

"Well, I got him out on fast balls high inside in those Florida games last spring," said Elmer McCaffrey.

"That was last spring. You pitch like I told you." Dave's manner was gentle but no one could doubt who was boss of the Dodgers. "Now this man Spike Johnson. Back in nineteen and thirty-one he was with me on the Senators. His first one is usually a fast ball. Then if he misses, he comes across with another; so if there's a man on base, lay onto that first pitch." He paused and the toothpick did its dance across his mouth. "Everyone get it?" He looked round. "Yes, Mike. . . ."

From the back of the room Mike Sweeney spoke up. He was the club scout, an old and canny ballplayer who had been following the Indians the last weeks of the season and was therefore listened to with respect. Heads turned in his direction.

"Jes' wanted to say, I been watching these boys pitch to Hammy lately. He shortens his grip on his bat when he's looking for a curve ball, so they don't throw him much he can hit. You can fool him with a change of pace, too."

"Okay, you pitchers. Get that?" He glanced again at the list in his hand. "Carey Thomas always wastes his fast ball. It's high and wide, so you can't get hold of it. He's been with the team since nineteen and thirty-three, so like Spike this is probably his last season. Likely they'll use him as relief if he does pitch. Wait him out, just wait him out; we'll get to him in three-four innings."

Funny how easy and relaxed Dave was. Might

have been playing a game in April. After all, though, it wasn't his first Series. Nor Fat Stuff's either, nor Rats Doyle's, both of whom wore World Series' rings. Nothing new to them, this business of two—maybe four—thousand extra in cash hanging on a few hits at the right time or a single error in the field.

The toothpick waggled in the mouth of the old catcher. "Jake, you played against this bird Miller; tell us 'bout him, will ya?"

Silence over the room. Somebody's spikes dragged nervously across the concrete floor. Someone else coughed. "Well, he sure is fast. Yessir! He leans back and pours that speed ball down the middle, and there isn't much you can do. Coupla years ago he had no curve. He's got a honey now, all right. Can hide it, too. Point is, when he comes from up here—" Jake Kennedy, the pitcher, stood up in the rear and everyone stretched to watch—"when it comes from up here . . . see . . . it's usually a fast ball. When it comes from here . . . it's likely a curve. But not always."

Everyone was talking. Everyone had seen him play one time or another. Yet everyone had a query. Without Miller the Indians were just another ballclub. Miller was the man to beat. If they could only lick that baby the Series was theirs. Four thousand instead of two thousand per man. It went through the mind of every single player in the room. All together they began bombarding Jake or Mike the scout.

"Like that man Murray of the Giants?"

"What's he throw with men on bases?"

"Is he really as fast as they say, Mike?"

"Listen," said the old scout. "He stands up there in the box and shows you a baseball, and then he winds up and reaches in his hip pocket and throws a pea to the plate."

"Well, can you bunt him?" asked someone.

"Bunt! Boy, he leans back and lets you have that fast one and there ain't nobody in a monkey suit can bunt it. You'll either miss it or it'll zip off for a foul strike. No siree; one way and another he don't figure to be any help a-tall with men on bases."

"Can't you dig in and hit him, Mike?"

"Jes' you try, Harry. A guy isn't gonna dig in very deep when he knows Gene might take the button off his cap with a fast one. First day I saw him pitch I went out and had my glasses changed. Sometimes I think no one can be that good and do those things I tell folks he's doing.

Then I watch him and doggone he's doing 'em before my eyes. He's a sweetheart, that baby."

From the rear of the room one player murmured something about signs. "Signs!" said the old scout. "Signs! Everyone in the league knows his signals. That don't make no difference. 'Course, if it isn't his fast ball, it's either his curve or his floater. You gotta be ready for any of them. And figure when it's on the way, too. Sometimes I scare myself, talking this way 'bout that boy. I wonder maybe if I'm not going nuts, and Heaven knows after the things I've gone through in baseball it wouldn't surprise me a bit. Not one bit. Then I sit up there and watch Miller, and I know it ain't me . . . it's him. He's a manager's dream and enough to make any old busher like me wonder is everything okay upstairs. . . ."

Dave interrupted. "Never mind signs, you fellas. You know I don't care much for sign stealing. Too easy to switch . . . then where are you? Now here's one thing. You Eddie on second, when Hank is chasing fouls, you foller that ball and yell to him where those stands jut out. The new box seats they just put in, I mean. Point is, he stopped ten feet short of those seats twice in practice yesterday. That might mean two putouts wasted . . . all the difference . . ."

"One thing more, boys. Keep your ears open. That's what God gave 'em to you for, remember. Listen to these-here-now newspapermen. Never mind any wisecracks, Razzle. You and Jake try and listen to someone else for a change, will ya? Don't forget, those boys have all talked with Baker and the Cleveland players. Sometimes they drop a hint that's mighty useful. Now this man Miller. Sure he's good; but he pulls his pants on one leg at a time same as you do. So just go out there and meet that ball. Tucker, I don't want you trying for homers. Get me a single, that's all I ask. Whatever you do, fellas, don't tighten up. Play your regular game and I know you can do it. Raz, you'll pitch; West will catch. All right, le's hustle every single minute, le's hustle out there on that field. . . ."

His final words were lost in a burst of noise. Chairs scraped on the floor, benches were shoved back. Spikes clattered. They didn't need to be urged. They were glad at last to be in it, to be moving. To be doing something, to have the blessed relief of action. As a unit they swarmed toward the door; clatter-clatter, clackety-clack, clackety-clack their spikes sounded on the concrete runway outside.

Dave Leonard rose from his chair, pulling at the sleeves of two men. The gang rushed through the door but they lingered with him. He put his arm round their shoulders. "Fat Stuff, I want you and Rats should watch these kids, the three of 'em—these rookies, Tucker and Street and Hank West. They're all as tight as drums and they're all in important spots. I dunno am I right in playing that boy West behind the plate; but with Babe's split thumb and my joints creaking there doesn't seem anything else to do. See if you can't loosen 'em up. If they come through, we'll win. We gotta take the pressure off or they'll play a bad Series. If Tucker could only get himself a hit this afternoon it would do him lots of good. You boys can pull them out of it maybe; if you see any way to loosen the tension, why . . ."

The two older men nodded. "Yep, we'll keep an eye on the kids, Dave."

"One thing more. Tucker had that bad accident against the fence in the Polo Grounds last week. Gave him a good shaking up. I'm scared he might be a little wee bit wall-shy in this first game. Fat Stuff, you go out there and hit some fungoes that'll back him clean up against that wall this morning. And, Rats, you sort of amble out into the field and watch him on the fence, will ya? See he don't get too close." The good-natured face of the old relief pitcher sobered up. He still recalled his first Series.

A Western Union messenger boy entered the big room, empty now save for the three men and Chiselbeak, the locker man, picking up discarded equipment and straightening out their clothes. The boy had a fistful of telegrams.

"Leonard . . . Case . . . Tucker . . . Dave Leonard . . . Stansworth . . . Roy Tucker . . . Leonard . . . Dave Leonard . . . Swanson . . ."

2

Clack, clack, clackety-clack, clackety-clack, clack-clack. Their spikes sounded the old familiar tune on the concrete walk leading to the field. But this was different.

Everything was different. Even the familiar diamond, shrouded in the strange light of early morning, was different. Usually they came out for practice about two in the afternoon; but the Series games started at one-thirty so now it was just after eleven. The field, as a rule so empty, was crowded, dotted with strange figures. There seemed to be hundreds of sportswriters, photographers, and men standing with their hands in their pockets talking to each other. Or just standing.

He walked to the dugout for his bat.

"Hey. . . . there's the Kid . . ."

"Hullo, Roy old boy . . . "

"Hi, Tuck, how are you feeling?"

"Hullo, Rex. 'Lo there, Sandy. I'm okay, thanks." Rex King of the *Times*, Sandy Martin of the *Post*, and several reporters who followed the team during the season crowded round. Was he over the effects of that crash into the Polo Ground walls? Any bones broken?

The Kid started to swing the two bats in his hand and looked around just in time to save a couple of curious onlookers from being beaned. "Naw, only a shaking-up, that's all. I'm fine."

"How's Stansworth?" asked a stranger, peering into the circle. The men he knew the Kid liked. But these others, the Cleveland writers and the rest he didn't know, were what made it all so different.

"Dunno. Better ask Leonard. The Babe's in uniform."

Then over their heads he saw the Indians slowly filing onto the field from the visitors' entrance. Instantly the circle about him dissolved. The Cleveland team seemed to him like mastodons. He thought he'd never seen such big men in monkey suits. The biggest of all was a young chap with enormous shoulders and long arms who was instantly surrounded by newspapermen.

That must be Miller, the guy they had to beat. Big, all right. Lots of power in those shoulders. He seemed loose and relaxed, laughing and joking with the Cleveland writers in the crowd.

Someone touched him on the arm. It was Jim Casey, the columnist. "Roy, I want you to meet Grantland Rice." A pleasant-faced, white-haired man was at his side.

"Glad to meet you, Mr. Rice." He looked at him curiously. The great Grantland Rice.

"How 'do, Tucker. How you feeling after that shake-up the other day? You sure took an awful tumble into that fence." His voice was soft and agreeable.

"Oh, I'm okay, thank you, Mr. Rice. I'll be in there playing ball this afternoon; leastways I hope so."

"Good enough. I bet Dave Leonard wishes the rest of the boys were like you . . . hey, Jim? Who's going to catch?"

"Dunno, sir. Guess Hank'll catch. Dave caught the most of that last game against the

Giants, but he said like he ached for two days afterward. Say . . . that man Miller, he's sure got power in those shoulders."

The others laughed. "Yep, he's a big chap, all right." The bell rang. Clang-clang, clang-clang. The Kid left them and went toward the batting cage, but before he got there someone stopped him.

"Mr. Tucker?" He held out a card.

"Yeah . . ."

"I'm from the J. W. Frost Agency in Detroit; largest agency west of the Hudson. You musta heard of us. We're anxious to get your endorsement on our new Colonel cigarette — maybe you've seen 'em advertised — the new ten cent brand."

The Kid turned the card over in his hand. "Uhuh." As a matter of fact he'd never heard of the agency and didn't know what kind of an agency it was, nor the cigarettes either. But it didn't seem polite to the stranger to say so.

"We're looking for you to do big things this week, Mr. Tucker. How you feeling?"

The Kid wasn't quite sure. All this difference, all these strange people, big shots like Granny Rice, the Cleveland writers, and now this chap, sort of made him uneasy. Nor did he like the man who was a little too smooth. "Who? Me? I'm all right. But looka here, I'm sorry, Mr. . . . Mr. . . ."

"Swan. Norman F. Swan of J. W. Frost. I'm a great fan; saw you play several times in Detroit this season." Now the Kid knew he was a phony. The Dodgers, being in the National League, had never played in Detroit. They'd played the Tigers a few practice games in Lakeland, in Florida; but never in Detroit. No, the man was a phony. He kept on confidently. "Oh, yes, the boys all know me. I just signed up Sammy Hammerstein and Gene Miller of the Indians; like to get one or two of you Dodgers, just to make it official, heh-heh . . . "

"Sorry; fact is I don't smoke."

The man threw back his head and laughed. While he was laughing the Kid wondered how he got on the field. Who let him on, anyhow? It made the Kid nervous; he was afraid someone standing near by back of the plate would hear the conversation. In any event, he didn't like the chap.

"Heh-heh! Say, heh-heh, that's good, that is." Men standing around turned curiously. "Don't smoke. Don't worry about that, Roy. Neither does Hammy, neither does Elmer Kennedy of the Sox or Sig Schecter of the Cardinals. Don't smoke . . . say, that's a scream!" He put one hand on the Kid's arm and yanked an official-looking document from his pocket.

"Just you sign here . . . on this line here . . . I witness your signature below . . . and you'll have a check for five hundred smackers round at your hotel tomorrow."

Now he was annoyed. This was baseball, a Series game, the *first* Series game. Why didn't they let a guy alone? "But I tell ya, I don't smoke. You want me to say I like those cigarettes of yours, don't ya . . . with my photo, and all. . . ."

"Sure! That's the idea, Roy. You don't hafta smoke 'em. Now that Whispies crowd, they tell me a man stands right over the boys and makes 'em eat the darn things. Yessir. We don't go in for foolishness of that sort. You sign here, and that's as far as . . ."

"No, thanks . . ."

"No, thanks what?"

"Just no, thanks."

"Why not?"

" 'Cause I don't smoke. That's why not."

A frown came over Mr. Swan's face. As an account executive of the J. W. Frost Agency he had met many strange types. But these ball-players sure were queer. Imagine a boy of nineteen holding up the agency that way. "Well, now, er . . . maybe we could . . . I mean . . . say, if you have a good Series . . . and it sure looks like you will . . . we might raise that . . . a little, say six fifty . . ."

Roy swung his bat. Gosh, how he'd like to smack it down on that expensive gray hat. "No, thanks." He turned toward the diamond where Harry Street, his roommate, was hitting balls over the fence.

"But, Mr. Tucker, here, wait a minute." The man grabbed him by the arm. "Wait just a minute; don't be so hasty about this. Let's say seven fifty. There! That's as far as I'm authorized to go. That's the limit. Seven fifty."

"Sorry. Nothing doing."

"You mean to say you'll chuck seven fifty smackers out the window because you don't happen to smoke?"

"I guess *so*. Anyhow, I'm not interested."

He walked away, the man following like a little dog, trying to hold on to his sleeve, to his arm. Roy stepped up to the plate.

He dug in his spikes, faced Speed Boy in the box who was tossing them up, took a toehold and put the wood on it cleanly. There! And there! And there! The balls sailed far, deep into the field. That was something like. It shook off the bad taste of that man from the J. W. Frost Agency. As he went back to the bench he saw him deep in conversation with one of the Indians.

Half an hour later Roy came back after fielding practice to the bench and watched the Indians run out.

Yessir, they were a good team. Nine old men . . . well, maybe. But they had lots of pep and ginger. And that second base combination was a dandy. Not as good as Harry and Ed; nosir, no one was as good as Harry and Ed. Those boys could get the ball away.

The stands covered with flags and bunting were filling up, and the swarm of reporters, radio men, and camera fiends on the field hadn't lessened either. Some of them sat on the bench surrounding Dave, kidding and joking with him. Dave laughed as if it was merely another game instead of one of the most important of the year.

Important to him, too, for if they won the Series he'd have a three-year contract as man-

ager. If not, well, if not . . . Taunton, maybe, or
Elmira, or maybe nothing. Dave was old. He
was forty, someone said. Yep, it was important, this game. If they got off to a good start,
they'd win. That's what Casey said, and all
the sportswriters. If you won the first; the team
that won the first game always won the Series.
So on the first game was the difference between two thousand and four thousand. He
thought of what it would mean; Grandma listening in on the farm, and the boys at the drugstore, and prob'ly old Mr. Haskins, the president of the First National Bank, who advised
him not to leave his job and go wasting his time
playing ball. Four thousand! Think what he
could do with that. Oil the road past the house,
bring in electricity from the state highway, get a
new oil burner for Grandma, and an electric
cookstove, maybe, and . . .

"What's that? Who? Miller starting for them?"
Someone was talking at the other end of the
bench.

"Yeah. Least that's what Sandy Martin says.
Says Casey said Baker told him so."

"Those ginks! What do they know?"

Back of home plate Razzle was warming up,
slowly, leisurely, as if this was just another

game. The Kid admired him, admired the way he rolled the ball round in his hand, glanced out over the diamond, lifted his head when someone yelled from the stands, and then burned the ball into his catcher's mitt. He was warming up all right, but so were Elmer McCaffrey and Rats Doyle.

A clown in a monkey suit with a dress coat over it and a battered silk hat appeared on the third base line. Cheers, especially from the bleachers. "Schacht!" Yes, it was Al Schacht, the famous baseball comedian, tripping, falling, stumbling through his act. The groundsmen were white-washing the batter's box, dusting off the infield.

Inside his stomach the Kid had the same sinking sensation he had the first time he came out to pitch at Ebbets Field. He suddenly wished that it was over. With all his heart he wished he was on the farm, back in MacKenzie's drugstore on South Main, in a Florida training camp; that he was any place anywhere save in that dugout.

The crowd seated above the big diamond, now empty save for Al Schacht going through his tricks, roared with delight as he ran to spear a liner, stumbled, and fell on his face. Even Harry on one side and Red Allen on the other laughed. The Kid couldn't. He was all tight inside.

". . . for Brooklyn . . . Nugent, No. 14, pitching. . . ." A roar from the stands. With Raz in the box, they couldn't lose. Razzle was the favorite of all Dodger fans. ". . . West, No. 18, catching. For Cleveland . . . Miller . . ." The roar rose again. So the big boy was going in. He was out there to win the first game . . . "and McCormick, No. 2, catching."

Somewhere a band began playing. Everyone stood, so the Kid stood, mechanically, without realizing it was "The Star-Spangled Banner." As the last note died away, a burst of chatter rose up and down the dugout. Dave stood facing them on the step.

"All right now, boys. Get out there and upset 'em. Hustle every minute, hustle. . . ."

Like a wave they jumped up the step and onto the sunny diamond. The stands rose, cheering. Well, here it was, two, four thousand. . . .

Once out in the field he felt better. The old familiar noises came to him through the haze of his concentration. "Score card . . . twenty-five cents . . . can't tell the players without a score card . . . anyone else wanta . . . popcorn and peanuts . . . five centsa . . . anyone else there . . . cold drinks, ice cold drinks . . . who wantsa ice cold . . . root beer, CocaCola . . . ." And the half-heard, half-understood shouts from the bleachers to his left, from the Knot Hole Gang, fans who had sat there through blazing summer heat and knew him for their friend.

Yep, it was something to start at home. And there in front were the same figures; Eddie Davis mechanically scooping up dirt in the basepaths, the broad back of Red Allen with the number 3 on it directly ahead, and the dancing figure of Jerry on the hot corner. And over all the noises and the chatter from the dugouts and the field came the voices of men he knew, voices he could pick out even in the crowd-roar as Razzle mowed down the batters . . . one . . . two . . . three. . . .

"Atta boy, atta boy, Raz, old boy old kid . . . tha's pitching . . . that is, Razzle . . . give 'em the old dipsy doo, Raz . . . ." "Hurry up . . . take yer time. . . ." Harry Street's favorite cry rose above the others as the side was out on a slow bounder to Eddie Davis and almost before he knew it half the inning was over.

"All right, gang, le's get us a run now. Roy, you're on deck."

Red Allen was up. The Kid watched the big

man in the box wind up, noticed his ease and grace, the smooth motion of his shoulder as he swung into the pitch, the tremendous speed as the ball smacked into the catcher's mitt.

Crack! A hit! Nope; just another can of corn.

The ball settled lazily into the center fielder's hand as Roy, swinging two bats, stepped to the plate.

Well, here goes. Whew! Fast! It was high, inside, but awfully fast. The old scout hadn't exaggerated. The big boy in the box shook off his catcher, half opening his mouth as he did so and exposing an empty space in front where a tooth was gone. Gosh, he was big; big as all outdoors. Ball two! Ah, that's it. Wait him out. The next one came . . . right across. He shouldn't have taken it. That was a dilly to hit.

Cracking the plate with his bat, the Kid pulled his cap down and took a good toehold. The ball came up, he swung . . . hit . . . and started for first, giving everything he had. But it was there before him. Slowly he walked back to the dugout.

"What's he got, Roy?" asked old Cassidy on the first base coaching line.

"He's got plenty, lemme tell you. Fast as they make 'em, that baby."

From the dugout came the chatter of the gang. "Save me a rap, Swanny. You can hit it, Swanny. All right, Swanny, old boy, this is the one . . . "

Swanson drew a base on balls. Miller had only one fault—he was inclined to be wild. Every speed merchant was, at times. The whole dugout leaned forward, while the crowd above yelled as Karl Case beat out a slow roller to third. Now Harry Street walked up to the plate. The Kid felt sorry for him. He realized the pressure on anyone facing baseball's best pitcher at that critical moment. Miller went to work on him as if it were the deciding run of the game. The big pitcher was determined to knock that rally in the head right there. A minute later, Harry struck out. Roy wasn't surprised. Very likely he himself would have done the same thing.

Up to the fourth inning it was a ball game. No one had scored or seemed likely to do so. Razzle was pouring in his best stuff, and Miller was in command for Cleveland. Then in the Brooklyn fourth the pitcher drew a base on balls. Maybe this was the inning. Behind the dugout the Dodger fans went wild, and on the baselines the coaches began shouting through cupped hands. You had the feeling this was the time. This was the start, the beginning of the end. Razzle on first and the top of the batting order up.

Allen tried to bunt. Foul, strike one. Shucks, why don't these birds take it from the old scout. Well, some folks just have to learn for themselves, that's all. Oh, boy . . . there she goes . . . that's a hit . . . go on, Raz you old ice cart . . . go on, you old elephant . . . go on, you . . . you . . . you truck horse . . . go on. . . .

The first real hit of the game. A clean single between second and first, to the right of the fielder. But Raz was too slow to make third. Anyhow, men on first and second and no one out as Roy came to bat. Now the stands were up. He could hear them calling his name, crying for a hit. Walking to the plate an idea came to him.

Why not give Miller the old gag? Pretend to take the first pitch, act as if he was going to let it go by, and then if it was good, sock it.

He stepped up carelessly, and instead of assuming his usual alert stance, stood waggling his bat, tugging at his cap, hitching his belt, and watching Charlie Draper on third for the signals. Miller shook off his catcher. That meant a fast one.

Boy, here goes that old ball game.

He tried hard to conceal his thoughts, to stand negligently at the plate as the big chap in the box drew himself up. Waiting till the last possible second he saw the ball leave Miller's hand and come on a line with his right shoulder.

Here it comes . . . I'll . . . no . . . it's too close to hit . . . I'll just turn and take it on my shoulder blades . . . get my base . . . here it comes . . . here . . .

Then ten feet from the plate the ball suddenly shot upward. He tried to shift, to move, to duck back; but his feet were locked.

BONG.

A bell rang in his head. It rang day and night for the next six weeks.

3

Harry was standing over him. And McCormick, the Indian catcher, his mask off. And old Stubblebeard the plate umpire. And Karl Case. Beaned! That was it. Beaned!

Someone was feeling the side of his head. No, not that side, not the left, the right side. Not the left, the right side. Nobody understood. Meanwhile, bong . . . bong . . . bong . . . bong . . . went that bell in his head.

He tried to get up. Someone pushed him back. Charlie Draper was supporting him. "Take it easy, Kid. Just take it easy now." Then he saw

Gene Miller, a queer frightened look on his face, peering down.

"Is he all right . . . is he all right? . . ."

Someone was hauling him onto a stretcher. A stretcher! Nuts to that! He wanted to take first, to run the bases, to get out there; and he tried to move. Three men on and nobody out. Three on and . . . "Hey, lemme get out there, will ya, you guys, lemme . . ."

Bong . . . bong . . . bong . . . gosh, he was dizzy.

"Take it easy, Roy, just take it easy." Yeah, take it easy. Maybe that was better after all.

The clubhouse was cool and darkish. Or was it the ice pack over his head as he lay stretched out on the rubbing table? The club doctor came in and began feeling his left temple and asking questions. Did that hurt there? There? Did that hurt?

"Not that side, Doc. Not that side. I bat left-handed, see. Not that side."

But the doctor continued feeling his left temple. No sense, these people. No sense at all.

Outside there was a sudden burst of noise. It kept on, louder, louder. Someone had scored. Must have been us. "Hey, Chiselbeak, what happened? Anyone score?" Where was that old dope? Never round when you wanted him.

A minute later the noise increased and before it died away there was a tremendous roar, a roar that grew and grew. A player came running in, his spikes clattering on the concrete.

"Gimme some tape, Chisel, quick. Ya, two bases on balls . . . an' Strong cracks a double down the left field line . . . I think they're yanking Miller now."

Yanking Miller! About time, if you ask me. Imagine, a gink like that, beaning men in a Series game.

Chisel came over to the table as the doctor left. "How ya feel, boy?"

"Kinda dizzy-like. And that bell, Chisel, can't you shut off that bell?"

"What bell?"

"That bell ringing. Don't you hear it?"

"Ain't no bell ringing. That's yer head, Roy. Take it easy, now. Just take it easy."

He pulled the ice pack off and started to replace it with a fresh one. As he did so a shadow in the door darkened the room for a second. A player was standing there; hot, sweaty, hair mussed up. He wore a Cleveland uniform.

They both saw him but it was the Kid who spoke.

"You . . . you . . . you Gene Miller . . . you call yourself a pitcher . . . why, you oughta be ashamed of yourself . . . you mug . . . you . . . a pitcher . . . that's been round as long as you have . . . and can't keep the ball over the plate . . . imagine, beaning a guy in a Series game . . . say, if I was you, I'd take off that uniform . . . you great big thug, call yourself a pitcher . . . listen, you bum you . . . if I was you . . ." For several minutes he went on, unable to stop, pouring out abuse on the distressed man in the door.

Miller never replied. Without saying a word he stood there, his big brown eyes open, his mouth twitching. Finally he turned and went away.

All the while Chiselbeak was patting him on the shoulder. "Now, boy, jest you take it easy; take it easy, Roy old boy. They'll be here with the ambulance in a minute."

The ambulance came. All night in the hospital he was hitting home runs and making impossible catches in the field. The next morning he was weak, and no wonder. But he felt better, more normal. Shortly after breakfast, which consisted of orange juice, the nurse said a man wanted particularly to see him.

It was Gene again. He stood trembling in the doorway. "Roy, gee, I'm sorry. Honest to goodness I didn't mean for to hit you, Roy. How are you this morning? Feel any better, do you? Say, I'm all busted up over this, honest I am, Roy. Please believe me, I hadn't any idea when I threw that ball . . ."

"Why, Gene, what you doing here? Of course I'm better. I'm okay now. Gene, don't you take on one little bit. I know you didn't do it on purpose. It was my own fault anyway; my feet were locked and I couldn't dodge back. Just one of those breaks, that's all. Everybody has to take 'em, so don't you worry about it, Gene. Don't you worry the least bit, hear me?"

His face lightened up. "You feel better, don't you, Kid? Sure 'nough?"

"Yeah, I feel better." He did, too. In fact he was sitting up for the first time without any dizziness. Only that continual bong-bong-bong-bong in his head. How long would that last? All day, maybe. "Yes, sir, you bet I am. And Gene. One thing. Don't pay attention to what I said in the clubhouse to you yesterday. I was wacky then. Understand? I was getting set to step into that one and you had a right to dust me off. I just didn't expect it, that's all. Understand?"

The big chap came over to the bed. He had a frank, open face, warm brown eyes, and when he smiled there was the gap in his teeth in front that made him look boyish—the same gap Roy had noticed when he came to bat. "Why, certainly, that's okay. I knew that, Roy, all the time. I knew you hardly realized what you were saying. Now get yourself well, hear me?" He leaned over. "Brought my radio along; thought you might like to get the play-by-play if you're stuck in here a few days."

The nurse poked her head in the door. "Your telephone, Mr. Tucker. Tomkinsville, Connecticut calling. Long distance wants you."

" 'Scuse me, Gene. That's my grandma, that is. She thinks I'm dead most likely. Hullo. Hullo there, Grandma . . . well, how are you? . . ."

All morning they had him in the X-ray room. Or so it seemed. Walk? No, he couldn't walk or at least they wouldn't let him, and he hated to be carried along on a stretcher. But they insisted. For an hour they took pictures of his head, his neck, his shoulders. From the top, from every

side, from all possible angles. Early in the afternoon a doctor in a long white coat came to exam-
ine him.

Patiently the Kid explained. Everyone seemed
to make the same mistake. "Nosir, you see I bat
left-handed, so the ball hit me here, on the right
side, not the left."

The man in the white coat paid no attention.
He kept on examining his left temple. "I know,
h'm. You're a mighty lucky young man, Mr.
Tucker. That was a close shave you had, a close
shave. It happened to be a glancing blow. The
ball didn't catch you full on the temple; it hit the
edge of your head as you turned and sheered off.
Had it struck full on, your skull would probably
have been fractured. You see when a man's skull
is fractured, it's broken on the opposite side
from where the ball strikes. Your left side is all
right."

That was it. That was why they all felt the
other side. He was cheered. "Yeah, but that big
knob there over my right ear. And the bell, doc.
Seems like I hear a bell ringing all the time."

Gingerly the doctor felt the bump on his right
temple. "H'm. That knob'll go down. Though in
all probability you'll carry some kind of bump to
your death-bed. But the ringing in your head is

quite normal. It'll disappear, little by little. All I can say is, you're an extremely lucky young man."

That was fine. But when would he be up and out and back there in the line-up? Those boys needed him. That was what he wanted to know, *and* Dave Leonard who came in for a few minutes, *and* the newspapers who kept calling all day, *and* the radio men, too. Telegrams poured in. Would he endorse the new Ripper bats? And Chesterfield neckties? And Wopsy-Cola, the new drink? Would he care to appear on the Cromium Steel Plate Hour for five hundred dollars? Seemed as if a man got more attention from being hit in the head than from hitting home runs on the field.

Directly the doctor left. He switched on Gene's radio. When he tuned in, it was nothing to nothing, start of the fourth, with Paul Drewes on the mound for Cleveland and Rats Doyle pitching for Brooklyn. One more victory would just about clinch things and Rats was the boy to do it. Two games to none would settle things.

". . . And it's deep, deep in left . . . yessir . . . it's over . . . I think it's over . . . yes, IT'S OVER THE FENCE . . . Over the fence in Bedford Avenue." A roar came from the radio. But the

John R. Tunis

roar chilled him. Who hit? Whose homer, you nitwit? What's the score there? His heart sank as he listened to the next three words. They told everything he needed to know.

"Lanahan and McClusky . . . going in . . . and old Hammy lumbering round second. He's turning third, and there's the whole doggone Indian team at the plate waiting to shake his hand. Yessir, that boy sure can powder that ball when he gets his wood on it. Four, no five to nothing, beginning of the seventh. Wonder will Dave Leonard yank Rats now?"

From his bed the Kid could see Dave sitting on the bench, his chin cupped in his hand, thinking to himself: "Well, Rats'll get the next man. He'll get the next batter. Rats is my first line pitcher. He'll get the next man. He'll get Hammy all right."

Then that homer.

". . . Yessir, like I told you, Leonard is yanking Doyle. Le's see who he'll put in; somebody's coming in from the bullpen . . . looks as if it might be Foster. Uhuh. Fat Stuff Foster, Leonard's handy man, coming in from the bullpen."

The Kid leaned across and switched the radio

37

off. Shutting his eyes he could see Fat Stuff waddling across the field, his long arms swinging by his side, as he had hurried to help in a dozen games all season. Now it was too late. You don't spot the Indians or any other first class club five runs and beat them in a couple of innings. Nope, you don't hand them a lead like that and catch them in a few whacks at the plate. One game apiece. Well, it wasn't a walkover. It was anyone's Series.

Half an hour later he turned on the radio just as the announcer was ending his description. "So on to Cleveland tomorrow, where it looks bad for the Dodgers. Leonard has used his star pitcher the first day, he's got a rookie catcher behind the plate, and he leaves Roy Tucker, one of his best hitters, in a hospital here in town. Last news we have is that Roy is coming on, but he'll have to stay several days for observation, and won't play again until the team gets back to Brooklyn on Thursday."

So that was it. The nurses in this hospital wouldn't tell you, the medicos wouldn't tell you, a man had to find out how he was from some darn radio announcer. Several days! Well, that was something. Better than being on his back all through the Series. He began to feel fine, like getting out once more. For a while he was so excited he almost forgot that steady ringing in his head. Bong-bong-bong-bong-bong went the bell.

4

Roy woke to the sound of rain pelting on a roof. He sat up quickly in bed, forgetting. A shock of pain went up the back of his neck. But it was raining. Raining hard. Maybe it would rain all day.

By noon it was still raining. Was it raining in Cleveland? He switched his radio on and twiddled the dial. ". . . And the third game of the World Series between the Brooklyn Dodgers and the Cleveland Indians to be held in Cleveland this afternoon was put off until tomorrow. The Dodgers won the first game, 6-1, and Cleveland the second, yesterday, 5-2."

Well, tomorrow was another day. And he was

better, no question about that. While the rain
descended on a dark and desolate city, he sat
up, even tried walking around the room without
much trouble. Only an occasional shoot of pain
up his neck, an occasional feeling of dizziness,
and that eternal bong-bong-bong in his head
reminded him of the beaning.

He hardly dared hope as he went to bed that it
would still be raining the next morning. But it
was! Never had rain meant so much to him,
never was it so welcome, and rain in his life as a
ballplayer was always pleasant to hear. Then the
same question: was it raining in Cleveland? It
was a long while before he could get any news on
the air. When he did there was the war in
Europe, an airplane accident in Utah, a robbery
in the Bronx. Finally the welcome words came.

"Judge Landis, with Managers Leonard of
Brooklyn and Baker of Cleveland, made an
inspection of the field just before noon today,
and following a conference decided to call off
the third game of the World Series scheduled
for this afternoon in that city. You remember
that the Dodgers won the first game by a score
of . . ."

Tomorrow. Maybe it would still be raining
tomorrow. Or the field wouldn't have dried suffi-

ciently. Maybe he'd be able to get out himself!
Late that afternoon the telephone rang. Dave
Leonard had been in communication with the
doctors at the hospital and told the Kid a place
had been reserved for him on the early Cleveland plane the next morning.

He reached the clubhouse just as the manager
was finishing his pre-game talk. Over their
heads he could see the old catcher, toothpick in
mouth, leaning across the back of a chair. " 'S I
say, we took too many balls in that last game.
We're not gonna take today. We'll beat those
birds at their own game, go out and hit 'em.
Everybody hit 'em. All right, le's go now." The
crowd turned toward the door to see the Kid
standing there, bag in hand. In a second he was
surrounded. They were glad to have him back
and their faces showed it.

"Hey, Roy . . . how are ya, Kid . . . here he is
now . . . glad to see you back again, Roy . . .
who said they could kill him off . . . boy, we
sure can use that old bat of yours right now . . .
c'm on, Roy, climb in the old monkey suit, we
can use you . . . how you feel, boy, okay?" A
dozen hands grasped his, a dozen arms reached
for his shoulder.

"Hullo, Fat Stuff, hullo, Raz old kid, hullo,

Dave, hullo, Harry. Hi there, Swanny. Hullo, Red. Sure I'm okay. Well . . . you know . . . little wobbly . . . that's natural the medicos say. But I'll be in there. . . ."

They left the room and went out. Clack-clack, clackety-clack, clack-clack, clackety-clack; the sound of their spikes on the concrete was sweet to his ears. He hurried off his clothes, half listening to the old catcher who paused a moment at his locker. "Roy, I shan't play you today. Want you should sit on that bench with me and try to size up this gang. We've got one tough fight on our hands and I'll need you before it's over. So take it easy. Don't run much. Moment you feel least bit dizzy, sit down. Keep outa the sun. Understand?"

He nodded. In half a minute he was grabbing his shoes. "Hullo, Chiselbeak. How are ya?" He laced them up. Clack-clack, clackety-clack on the concrete tunnel to the dugout. Crunch-crunch on the wooden planks of the dugout floor. He looked round. Whew! Say, this was a ballpark. This was big, this stadium was. A different park and a different scene. But still the same old sounds of baseball. The get-'em-red-hot of the dog men, the program vendors, the shouts of the crowd from the stands, all the sounds of baseball; sounds he only half heard but recognized now coming back to them again. Someone stopped him. A man presented an autographed baseball and a fountain pen.

"Oh . . ." he looked at the signature. "You're Tucker, hey? Thought you was beaned in Brooklyn!" He eyed him suspiciously. Roy grinned and said nothing. You can't please some folks, as Dave always said.

Gosh though, it was great to be back. To watch Harry with that familiar gesture knock the dirt from his spikes with a bat, to see Dave in his crouch at the plate tip his mask and take a high inside one from the pitcher, and Red Allen swinging those two war clubs. Yes, it was swell to be back. Back with the team, with men he loved. He felt he couldn't stand sitting all day in the dugout. Then he jumped instinctively to avoid a foul and got that twinge in the back of his neck. While all the time the bong-bong-bong went on in his head.

"Hey Roy!" Eddie Davis stopped on his way to the plate. "D'ja see what Casey called you in his column? He called you 'Wooden-Head Tucker.' Says you tried to use your nut for a bat."

"Yeah? Well, I wish it hada been Casey out there. Just let him stick his neck in front of Miller's fast one and he'll find out how wooden . . ."

A hand gripped his arm. It was a hand of steel. He turned about and looked into the freckled face of an older man. He had sandy hair parted on one side and blue eyes with crinkles at the corners.

"Listen, boy! Don't pay any attention to that man Casey, hear me?" As he talked he emphasized his remarks by taps on the Kid's arm with his other hand.

"Hullo, Mr. MacManus." It was Jack MacManus, owner of the Dodgers, one of the smartest men in baseball. Everyone knew Jack's heart was set on a Series title and usually he got what he went after.

"That man Casey! Lemme tell you. He always has to ride someone. That's the sort of sportswriter he is. Don't let him bother you. If you do, and he thinks it worries you, he'll wisecrack you to death every morning. I know. I had several run-ins with that baby when I was in Chicago. Get me?"

"Sure do. And thanks lots, Mr. MacManus."

"How you feel? Didn't expect that high inside one on the first pitch there, did you?"

"Nosir. But I'm better now. Awful glad to be back."

"And I'm mighty glad to have you. We can use that old mahogany of yours out there at the plate, Roy. Watch yourself, now." He turned away. Soon the familiar voice of the announcer came through the loudspeaker above.

"For Cleveland . . . Thomas, No. 19, pitching; McCormick, No. 2, catching. For Brooklyn, McCaffrey, No. 11, pitching; West, No. 18, catching."

He saw Dave beckoning and squeezed into a place at his side. Up and down the bench rang the chatter of the jockeys trying to ride the Indian pitcher. This was the game they wanted, the game which would put them once more in the lead.

That afternoon the Kid felt he learned as much baseball sitting beside Dave Leonard as he had learned all season. It was a pitcher's battle, with each manager hoping to wear down the other hurler. Thomas was an old timer, smart, keen, with a team of quick thinkers behind him. Sitting quietly in the dugout as a spectator, Roy could appreciate the skill of the man in the box, watch his strategy and that of the men in the field. As a non-combatant from the dugout, things were different. From the dugout the pitcher's mound really was a mound, and sitting on the scarred wooden step you saw things a man missed when he was playing. Closely he watched Dave shift his fielders around for each batter, trying to outguess them. Things were moving in the first inning.

Red Allen hit a sizzling grounder at Lanahan in short. The Indian player was slow getting it away, and the batter was safe at first. "Huh! The old fella's slowing up. Harry'd have had that one in his pocket."

Dave was an old timer himself. He came to the veteran's defense. "Yeah, yeah, maybe so. But he's still one of the best fielding shortstops in the league and still able to pull 'em out of the bag." The next Dodger smacked a hit over second. That is, it was going over second. Somehow Lanahan got there, deflected it toward Gardiner who scooped it up and shot it back to him in time for the force-out. "See! What'd I tell you? He's an old player, he forgets his errors once they are made. Put it out of your mind. If you make a bumble, Roy, forget it. Don't hang on to it. Don't let your mistakes get you down. We all make 'em."

The Kid, however, was loyal to his teammates.

"Harry and Eddie would have had that ball, too. Likely they'd have had a doubleplay out of it, even."

"They'd have tried for it, maybe. Point is, experienced men don't always try for a double. They want to be sure of getting the man at second. Youngsters might have tried for a double on that play; they'd have probably fumbled the ball and then where would you be? Everybody safe, see?"

Yes, he saw. He saw there was lots to baseball he didn't know, even if he was playing on a pennant winner. It was strange to be sitting there, watching his team from the dugout and not from his spot in deep right. To see Red Allen astride the bag and not his back with the big number 3 on it; to notice the changes in Elmer's face in the box; and have Harry's "Hurry up . . . take yer time . . ." come sharp and clear across the diamond. Strangest of all was to watch his substitute, Paul Roth, out in right. He could see the man clench and unclench his fists, and the tenseness of his movements as he snapped his sunglasses back on his cap after a foul to the stands. It made him restless to watch them out there fighting without him.

"Dave, I'd sure like to be out in that ball game with the boys."

"Yeah, I know how you feel. I remember when I was hurt in the Series in nineteen and thirty-five. Don't you worry, boy, you'll get lots of chance to play. It won't be over tonight . . . looka that!" Disgust and disappointment were in his voice. "Another pop-up. Those boys are all tightened up. They're gripping too hard. Harry . . . go get us a hit there, will ya?"

From the dugout the Kid watched the eternal duel of baseball, the thing that made it the greatest of games, the struggle of wits between the man at the plate and the man on the mound. Though he was pulling for a hit, he none the less found it exciting to watch old Thomas fool with the batters. Zwoosh. A fast ball under the chinstraps which rocked the shortstop back on his heels. Sizzz . . . a curve on the outer edge for a called strike. Zoom . . . a fast ball, high, with Harry swinging helplessly underneath it. Then one down by the knees, too low to hit. Finally the pay-off, the No. 2 pitch. By this time Harry was completely tied up. He took a half-swing and up went an easy pop to the infield.

"Yessir, he's a pitcher. He's a ballplayer's ballplayer, that lad Thomas," said Dave as the teams changed sides in the third without any scoring. The Kid who had looked on this pitcher as a has-been, as easy pickings, began to have respect for his knowledge and skill. Say, if Red couldn't hit him, nor Harry, nor Swanny either, he'd better stay right on this bench.

"Who's up?" he asked mechanically.

"McClusky," said Dave without even glancing at the plate. How did he remember? Then the Kid reflected that it was part of Dave's job to remember; and his own, too. Sure enough, the tall figure of the Cleveland center fielder came out of the dugout.

"There's a sweet young ballplayer. And gonna be better. Notice he's copied his swing from old Gardiner? See, he holds his bat the same as Gardiner." No, the Kid hadn't noticed. Dave saw just about everything.

On the first pitch the batter hit a single to left. Dave shook his head. "That's smart thinking up there. D'ja notice that? He set Elmer up. See, he's taken every first pitch since we started the Series. Then today he gets Elmer carelesslike, and when he puts it in there, McClusky hits it. Gotta give him credit. That's percentage base-ball."

And a minute later. "Ah . . . I knew he'd do

that. I told Hank to watch 'em. He's too tight."
It was the second pitch. As the catcher drew
back to return the ball to the pitcher, McClusky
on first dashed for second. Ed Davis was kicking up dirt way back of the infield, Harry was
flatfooted on the grass behind short, and the bag
completely open.

The crowd roared while Dave smacked his leg
with annoyance. "I told that boy; yessir, I told
that boy," he muttered, half to himself. "Always
do it on a rookie catcher. I oughta be in there
myself."

From the dugout they watched Gardiner, the
veteran second baseman, come to bat. "He'll
bunt."

"Nope, he won't."

"Why not? It's good baseball here."

"That's why. It's good technical baseball;
but likely he'll cross Elmer up. Or try to.
There . . . now . . . see?"

A smartly hit ball almost took the pitcher's ear
off as it sizzled over second. McClusky was
rounding third going in, with the stands on their
feet yelling. He slid into the plate in a flurry of
dust to score the first run of the game. Back of
the box Harry took the throw-in, preventing
Gardiner from reaching second.

"That's tough. Now see, get this, Roy. That one mistake there of West's may cost us the game. The way these two boys are throwing, one run may win for 'em. Shoot, he was off his toes once, and there goes your ball game. Mind you, it wasn't as if I hadn't warned him. I told him. Good teams always try to run bases on a rookie catcher, I told him yesterday. Forgot to mention it this morning."

Roy said nothing. There was nothing to say. He was learning baseball, about which he considered he knew something. Now he saw it all differently; from the angle of the manager. From the bench where a man watched and suffered while other men he had taught and trained and coached all season made mistakes before his eyes; mistakes that would cost a game, maybe a Series, maybe a couple of thousand dollars to every player on the squad.

The old catcher shook his head. He broke off a piece of gum. "Well, that's baseball." The crowd was yelling as Hammy hit a double down the right field line, and the inning ended with two runs scored.

Now the dugout was crowded with sweating, panting figures. "Hank, what were you doing out there, going fishing?" Dave leaned down the bench toward his young catcher.

The boy shook his head. "That was bad, Dave. I just didn't see him going down."

"But, Hank, suppose a man went down every time. You gotta imagine a man is stealing on every play. Now then, gang, some runs."

"Yep, c'mon gang, le's us get some runs."

Everyone was talking. "Naw, that was my fault. I never covered the bag; I was asleep . . . they got all the luck, them babies . . . luck my eye, that's quick thinking . . . well, I call it luck . . . he said this was a fast-ball league; I ain't seen many fast balls up there. . . naw, he's chucking curves . . . we'll get them back, gang, and more, too. What say, boys, le's get some runs ourselves. . . ."

But Dave knew and the team knew, though no one mentioned it, that there was all the difference between a one and a two run lead. Those two runs made the Indians cocky. It gave them heart and fight and confidence. On the other hand, being two runs behind put pressure on the Dodger hitters. They were up there swinging, trying too hard, too anxious to get a hit. Take it easy, boys, take it easy. Only a chap didn't take it easy. He tightened up.

Inning after inning went by with man after man slinging down his bat and coming into the dugout muttering. Still Carey Thomas refused to weaken. His skill had the Dodgers always going after a bad ball.

"He's a little gink, too. Not big like Miller, with shoulders. Where the blazes does he get all that power?"

"Yeah, he's little, but he's sure got a hook in there. He can break it three feet when he wants to. Now then . . . here's our chance, boys. This guy's a seven inning pitcher, he is. Le's get to him."

Was Thomas slipping? The first man up in the eighth got a base on balls. Hank West stepped to the plate while the dugout rang. "Put the wood on it, Hank . . . here we go, fellas . . . there's the one you want, Hank old kid . . . YEAH . . ." And the runners were off. Ed Davis on first rounded second, slid into third, while Hank West took second with a desperate slide. Second and third; no one down. The whole team was on the step, yelling through their hands. This was the old fight. They were coming from behind, they were going to slug their way as they had so many times all season. Yes, this was the moment. Now they were off. The coaches on the bases held up their hands. No one out. Ah. . .

Now it was the turn of the Cleveland crowd to roar. A pop-up to the catcher. Shucks! Well, only one down. Then the stands went wild. Tired, weary, Carey Thomas, giving everything he had, struck out the next batter. Suddenly the Kid heard those words from Dave at his side. He could hardly believe it.

"Roy! Go up there and see what you can do." Already Paul Roth had started for the plate. Roy jumped. He went over for his favorite bat and shuffled out of the dugout. A ripple of sound came down from the packed stands; it became louder and louder. He touched his cap. Then silence. Would he be plate-shy, he wondered, as he heard his name called? The Cleveland catcher spoke to him.

"Hullo, Tucker. How ya feel? Okay?"

"Sure." He rapped his bat against the plate.

"Tucker, No. 34, batting for Roth, No. 31."

The little man in the box looked tired. He yanked mechanically at his cap and hitched at his trousers. As he turned and went back to the rubber, the Kid could see a big sweat patch around the crotch. That guy's nearly all in. I can hit him. I must hit. . . .

"Strike one. . . ." Right down the middle. And the bat never left his shoulder. Gee whiz he'd expected a curve.

"Strike two!" Hang it! A roar from the stands. That was a dandy, too. On the bases Hank West and Ed Davis shouted at him. The coaches yelled words he couldn't hear, and from the dugout behind came a machine gun fire of encouragement. "You can do it, Roy old boy, only takes one . . . that don't mean a thing . . . now, Roy, lean into it . . . powder that pill, Roy . . . just give us a single, that's all we need, Roy, give us a single, will ya? . . ."

But he was jittery. He felt jittery. He knew he was jittery and tried to settle down, to control himself, to concentrate upon the ball. A curve? No, the next one would be a fast ball. Yep, this would be a fast ball. He stood waiting. The ball came . . . he swung hard, swung himself clean off his heels. The ball plunked into the catcher's mitt.

•

Dave was sitting in his suite in the Hotel Cleveland that night after dinner. Round the table were Draper, Cassidy, and Mike Sweeney the scout; his brain trust. One of his jobs as manager each night was to go over the batting order of the opposing team, check on their hitting averages, and make such changes in his pitching orders as were indicated. Thus, on seeing that Hammy was hitting .375, he made a note to tell the pitchers the next morning to try something else on the big first baseman. In the middle of their conference the telephone rang.

"Yep. Talking. Who's calling? Philadelphia. Put her on. Hullo . . . hullo, Helen. How are you, dear? Sure we're disappointed . . . that was a tough one to lose. Well, the boys are in a slump. The hawks have got 'em . . . I say the hawks have got 'em, they can't do nothing right. What's that? No one knows why, it's like that. You can't explain slumps. Oh, sure, they'll shake out of it . . . next Christmas, maybe . . ." There was anxiety in his tone, and the bitterness of a man who had things bottled up and needed to let them go. To the team he could never betray lack of confidence. To her he talked as he felt.

"Well, we'll all be out there trying again tomorrow. What say? No, ma'am, we aren't licked yet, not by a long shot. Uhuh. Uhuh. Why, there's enough managers round the lobby looking for jobs to fill that there stadium . . . uhuh . . . you bet . . . yep . . . all right . . . all right, dear . . . I'll call you tomorrow . . . all right . . . g'by. . . ."

He rang off and turned back to the brain trust round the table. "Wants to know what makes slumps. Why the hawks get 'em. I wish you'd tell me. Now, boys, sure as God made little apples he'll pitch Miller tomorrow. With three, no, four days' rest, that big boy will be ready to go. I figure like we should . . . "

5

The locker room was quiet and empty save for Chiselbeak stepping round, his arms full of clothes, and the Doc leaning against the rubbing table in his alcove. In an hour he would be the busiest man in Cleveland with sore ankles to tape, bruises to patch up, and inflamed muscles to soothe; but now, dressed in white trousers and a white undershirt, he stood with folded arms listening to a portable radio on his table. There was a sound of spikes on the concrete outside. Not the cheery clack-clack, clackety-clack as they took the field. No, a slower, mournful sound.

Clack . . . clack . . . clack-clack . . . clack . . .

The door opened and Razzle entered. His cap was at a despairing angle on the back of his head, his glove jammed into his hip pocket, his shirt soaking wet, his face covered with moisture. Doc turned his back and suddenly became busy with the liniments on his table. Chiselbeak bustled from locker to locker, hanging up clothes. Neither said a word as the big pitcher moved across the room and slumped down before his locker. What was there to say?

At last Razzle sighed. A heavy sigh, the sigh of disappointment and fatigue combined. He looked around, addressing Chiselbeak across the room who was the only person addressable.

"Tha's baseball for you. You get all ready . . . you feel fine . . . you have your stuff . . . and then what? They tee off on you. Gimme a Coke, Chisel.

"Thanks. Gosh, I'm tired! Funny how tired a man is when they hit you. Three innings and I feel like I pitched thirty-three. Yeah, they hit me. They sure did. Doc, I'm telling you . . ." The Doc now stood in the doorway of his alcove. "Doc, I'm telling you I had everything I ever had. I was fast and I was putting that ball right in there where I wanted. Still they kept a-hitting everything I had. You can ask Hank West if I didn't have plenty on the ball. Just ask Hank when he comes in."

"Cheer up, Razzle. You'll get another whack at them."

"Uhuh. You bet. Say, you know how much I wanted to win, don't you, Doc? But the real reason, believe me, the real reason I wanted to win was for Dave Leonard. He's one swell fella, and he's gotta be back with us next year. I'm afraid he won't be unless we take this Series. That gink MacManus plays with winners only. I heard he was talking with Scotter of K. C. last night. Shoot! I feel pretty bad, letting Dave down. Wouldn't be any fun playing under some other manager. He's a white man, he is."

"You didn't let him down."

"I did so. Well, there's no telling in baseball. The other day in Brooklyn we knock Miller out and I give three hits. So far we ain't got but two hits off him and they knocked me out. Tha's baseball." He pulled off his sweaty undershirt. "Gimme another Coke, Chiselbeak. Now take that hit Painter made. It was half off the handle of his bat. Absolutely. And I never threw a better pitch in my life than the one Gardiner got to." From outside came a roar, sudden, sharp. "Hope that means we're getting a few base knocks ourselves. Just because they run me out of there doesn't say we have to lose, even if Miller is pitching."

It was a dark gray afternoon on the field, ideal for a fast-ball pitcher. Dave looked over at the movement in their dugout. Why, that bird was throwing to Swanny and our best hitters as if he owned 'em. And Casey or someone said Miller wouldn't be any good the rest of the Series after beaning Tucker! Shucks! With three runs across and Brooklyn's best pitcher in the showers, the Cleveland stands were jubilant and the players loose and chattering. Easy to be loose and snappy when you're two games to one ahead and have a commanding lead in the fourth. When a pitcher gets a three run lead he can be more deliberate, he doesn't have to be so fine with the batters, he isn't so likely to get into a hole. Dave glanced anxiously at right field. Hold up both hands, Roy, if you feel one of those dizzy spells coming. Don't forget. Hang it, that's the difference between being ahead of the batters or behind them. When a pitcher's ahead of them like this baby, the hitters always choke their swing. Always.

Maybe so, he thought as he sat there on the bench, maybe so, but what can you do? Can't go up there and hit for 'em. But why not? He couldn't hit any worse than some of those boys. Then he saw how ridiculous the idea was. In the Series at forty. Life begins at forty. The Series begins at forty. He foresaw the cracks that Casey and the sportswriters would make. But he needed to do something to loosen the team. If only Babe Stansworth's thumb healed, they'd have at least one dependable hitter. Babe never choked, never. However, his thumb was not healed and wouldn't be in time to play, either. Yet something must be done. Soon.

There was a close decision on first and a Cleveland runner was called safe. Instantly Jake Kennedy threw his glove down in the box and started for old Stubblebeard, the umpire on the bag. He was followed across the diamond by Jerry Strong and Harry Street. Ed Davis ran over from second. Dave knew the symptoms. The pitcher was nervous, beginning to realize he didn't have much on the ball. Breaks were going against him and he was losing confidence. His nerves were giving way. The others also were jittery. Got to pull those boys together somehow.

Maybe they'd loosen up if they could only have a real good scrap.

With the score card in his hand he shifted Swanny in center. The next batter lined a sizzler right at him. Well, that was something. Anxiously he glanced at the Kid in right. His first game; would he last all right? Hold up your hands, Roy, if you get one of those dizzy spells. Yep, but would the Kid remember in the excitement of play? There! Three out! Now boys . . .

Once again the dugout was alive. "Where's my bat? No, not that. Gimme Betsy. All right, what say, fellas? How 'bout us getting some runs . . . this is our inning, this is. Okay, boys, watch for the fast ones and the curves won't fool you . . . Dunno what's the matter with me. He's the same pitcher I hit all over the park in Brooklyn and I can't see him today . . . why, he was out a foot. A foot, I tell you. Wasn't he . . . wasn't he, Dave?"

"I dunno, Jake," answered Dave, his eyes and his concentration on the plate. "I was ninety feet away; you were twenty. Now, boys, what say we go. . . ."

•

The glib voice of the announcer came into the

cool living room. Before the radio sat the three of them listening to their future unfold itself play by play. Even the two girls, wide-eyed, knew what hung in the balance. They were a ball-player's daughters, and they felt and understood the troubled look on their mother's face. Maybe Daddy'd have a job next year. Maybe he'd be manager of the Dodgers again. But maybe not.

". . . Here we go, folks. . . into the last of the sixth . . . still four to one in favor of the Indians. And the way Gene Miller is going now, looks as if he'd handcuff the Dodgers."

"Mummy, maybe they'd better put Daddy in there. Can Daddy put himself in to play, Mummy?"

"Sssh." Well, it wasn't so silly at that! Dave would surely do no worse than most of them.

". . . And so coming into the last half of the sixth, Gene Miller himself is up . . . hear that reception . . . hear that hand the crowd is giving the big chap. He tips his cap as he steps to the plate . . . this is his first winning game. He pitched the opener in Brooklyn, you remember, and was knocked from the box after he'd beaned Roy Tucker. . . ."

●

Out in deep right the Kid had watched Razzle,

Razzle the mighty, Razzle the triumphant, who had won twenty-two games for them during the season, who had beaten Miller in Brooklyn, trudge across to the showers. His shoulders were slumped. His usual cocky demeanor had gone.

Razzle, that's tough, that's tough, old boy. Razzle hasn't got his stuff today. Some of his folks in the stands there, too, and his girl. Well, that's baseball. Listen to those fans give him the razoo. Listen to 'em. As Fat Stuff says, a fan's a fan. He pays his dough to yell and criticize.

"All right there, Jake old boy, let's get this man, old kid." He whirled his arm three or four times to loosen it up, to help with his throw if needed. Gotta be on your toes in this man's game. Razzle out. 'N I'm not doing so good, myself, either. Hope Dave doesn't yank me . . . there it goes. . . .

The ball was hit deep to Karl Case in left, a long hit. Foul! Nosir. Struck the foul line. Gosh! Are they gonna have all the breaks? Man on second and nobody down. That sure is a tough one. Well, we can come from behind. We can hustle, take chances on the bases, come from behind and win. We've done it all season.

"Tha's chucking, Jake, that's the old stuff.

Pour in that old sinker on him, Jake-boy. He'll swing on this one."

A smart grounder to Jerry Strong behind third. The baseman with the ball in his hands feinted to second, sent the runner diving back for the bag, and then with a beautiful low throw nipped the batter at first by inches.

Say! There's a play for you! If only we all were doing as well as Jerry. He's dependable, that man. Yes, and he's under-rated as a ball-player because he isn't flashy. I sure know that.

"All right. One down, Jake. One down, le's go after this man, Jake old kid."

Hullo, here's their catcher. They're ahead; there's only one thing to do, dump it. He won't hit. So I'll shorten up a little. But I won't break till he shifts his feet to bunt. Watch his feet, Dave says, watch his feet. There she is . . . doggone, he crossed us . . . he hit it. . . .

"Yours, Swanny, Swanny . . . Swanny . . . all yours, Swanny. . . ."

Duck soup. Well, two down. I'll just give that old arm a coupla swings again. They'll hafta hit now. If they give me a chance I'll sure throw that man on second out, yessir I will. I think my throwing arm's better than Swanny's. It helps a chap to have been a pitcher, no use talking. Yessir, I'd like a chance to throw that man out.

•

Into Grandma's big living room on the farm where Roy had been born and brought up, a voice came sharply. ". . . And that was an error, a bad error for right fielder Roy Tucker. He misjudged that hit . . . and there goes Lanahan across the plate with the fifth run, and Hammy takes second on Swanson's throw in. That was an error; he misjudged that hit or maybe he lost it in the sun. Just stood there with both hands up and then sort of stumbled around while Swanson chased it. That makes five to one for Cleveland, two men out, the end of the sixth. . . ."

She leaned over and snapped off the radio, adjusting her spectacles. Then she looked up at Rafe, the hired man, who was standing beside her. "It's an outrage, playing Roy like that so soon after his accident. You'd think folks would know better. What do you suppose the doctors were thinking about? He should have spent a week in bed. I wish I had him home here right now, I declare I do. Doesn't matter how much money he's making if he ruins his health trying to play baseball. My goodness sakes alive, there's the water boiling."

Grandma was having tea, straight black tea, to comfort herself. When Grandma drank her tea straight in the afternoon it was as if Razzle had been taking beer for dinner without permission. Things had gone as far as she could stand.

•

He came in from the field and went to the bench. Dave said nothing about his mistake; probably that would come later. The dizzy spell had passed, but to make sure he washed his face and hands in ammonia and ice water. Then he dried them with a towel, rubbed rosin on his fingers, wiped them clean again, and dabbed his eyes with a little cold water. "By gosh, I'm gonna hit this time," he kept repeating to himself.

C'mon somebody, just pick me up this once. C'mon, Hank. Let's see, we're three, no, four runs behind. Hard to get in the ninth, though we've done it before. Another foul. Shoot! Say, that pitcher's all right; looks like we underestimated him the other day. Guess he's all they said about him last week. But this game isn't over yet. Nosir, not until the last man's out.

Get on there, Jake, just get on, that's all. The boys below me have picked me up lots this year; maybe they'll get going, too. Watch it, Jake, he's been feeding you low balls. Just lay onto one, kid.

Wow . . . oh, say! Is that baby lucky, that Miller. That ball sure was tagged. Then he sticks up his glove, and whang! There it is.

Jake passed him on his way to the dugout. "Tough luck, old kid."

"Yeah, well, you can only hit 'em. You can't steer 'em after they're hit," rejoined the pitcher philosophically.

"Here, boy, gimme that club. I'm gonna rap one. Red is saving me a rap." The Kid stepped out into the circle. The sun had come out half way through the game, but the circle and the diamond were now in shadow. In the field the Indians were whipping the ball around the bases with the dash and confidence that only can come to a winning team far in the lead.

On one knee he leaned over his bat. Just get on, Red, I'll bring you in; so help me I'll bring you in, boy. We'll start something, you and I, Red; we'll start things like we did that day in St. Louis. And the time we beat the Cubs in the tenth with two down and three runs to get. Look at those fans. They aren't leaving. They know we're a dangerous bunch until the last man's out, the fans do. We can get a run, three-four runs. We need five, but we'll settle for four. Give us a single, Red, just a single.

The stands rose. At the plate the batter leaned hard into the ball, struck it cleanly, and started for first. A deep one, far back, back; but the fielder was moving swiftly with the crack of the bat and was under it as it fell. One more routine catch. And another game gone. The Kid hit the ground hard with his bat, slung it away, and started toward the player's entrance.

Across the ballpark the Indians scuttled hastily for the clubhouse as the fans poured down upon them. No one poured down on the Dodgers, nobody mobbed them or pestered them for autographs. They were a beaten team. A few curiosity seekers trudged along, but mostly they were left to themselves. Silently save for their pants and grunts they trooped inside. Even Charlie Draper, holding the big leather ball bag, carried it at a disconsolate angle.

Shucks, thought the Kid. Why didn't he save me a rap? I shouldn't be kicking though; I didn't do much to help today myself. Muffed a bad chance in the field and went four times without a hit. Four horse collars. Maybe I swung too hard. It couldn't be that shadow there, I been hitting in shadow all season. Yes, sir, that bird Miller is all the old scout said he was. Now I wish I'd paid more attention to him that morning. You gotta hand it to Miller though; he's plenty pitcher, that baby.

Within the locker room was Razzle, all dressed, astride a corner bench. His usual after-game cigar was in his mouth, but it was not at his usual jaunty angle. Everyone felt the defeat badly. They trooped in, slumped down on the stools before their lockers, speechless. A few called for Cokes. The majority shook their heads and sat silently. In the dressing room of the manager, Dave and the coaches were taking off their clothes. Before Dave had got far he was surrounded by reporters. He sat on a chair, pulling off his socks, his pants.

"Good Lord, what you birds want? You should be over there talking to Baker."

"We were. Got anything to say, Dave?"

"What is there to say? Those babies hit everything we threw up to the plate. Hammy swung on a pitch that was six inches inside and knocked it into right for that single that scored their first run.

"How 'bout Stansworth? Any chance of his playing? Are you satisfied with West?"

"I gotta be satisfied with him, haven't I? Who've I got to take his place? Lost my relief catcher last month, and then Babe Stansworth splits his thumb wide open last week. You can't expect a man to catch when he has a split down the side of his bare thumb, can you?" The usually mild Dave glared at the questioner. He was tired and discouraged and in all the crowd he was the one who couldn't show discouragement.

"Care to name your starter tomorrow?"

"What's that? Nope, I dunno who'll pitch tomorrow's game. Your guess is as good as mine." He turned his back and threw wet clothes to the bench. In a minute he left them and went to the showers. The reporters came into the big room and mingled among the players, now recovering and starting to talk.

"Whatsa matter, Razzle? Tired out from three innings?"

"Nope. Not now." The big fellow uncoiled his long legs. "I just didn't have my stuff today. My curve ball hung there and I couldn't get my fast one by 'em. They hit everything I threw up."

"Say . . . was Miller using a lot of trick stuff,

Swanny?" asked Casey, a pencil and a pad in his hand.

"Trick stuff! With that four run lead. Why, he could ha' thrown anything."

"You sure can't win if you don't hit and score runs," said someone across the room.

"Shoot," came back the answer. "We never once got a break. Those Indians had all the breaks. Tomorrow they'll need 'em and they won't get 'em. Wait and see."

"Jes' so Miller don't pitch tomorrow, that's all I ask," retorted Case.

"Yeah. He sure pitched a darn fine game. But what in blazes, we've only made eight hits the last two games. We're better'n that. We're due for a change."

"Say, I don't mind going hitless myself so long as we can win."

"Well, we won the hard way all season. We came from behind to grab off the pennant; we'll pull out the Series, wait and see."

"Anyhow, you'll split eighty-two thousand. That's the take they gave out this afternoon for the first four games," said Casey. "And eighty-two thousand isn't hay."

A chorus of rebuffs rose all over the room.

"I wanna win."

"So do I."

"Me, too."

"That's right. We gotta win this-here Series. We haven't played our game yet, least except that first one."

"Yessir, we're better than anything we showed so far."

Roy said nothing. He pulled off his wet clothes, tired, unhappy. Bong-bong-bong-bong went the bell in his head. So tense had he been he'd hardly noticed it out there in the field. He noticed it now, all right. Climbing out of his sticky undershirt he went across into the soothing warmth of the showers. The hot spray beat on his aching legs and back. Ah . . . that was something like. No shouts, yells, or laughter came across the partitions. The others too were beaten and exhausted. Funny, he thought to himself, how much more tired a man is when he's played in a losing game.

Slowly he put on his clothes. After finishing he went over to Chiselbeak and handed him the key to his locker in the valuables trunk. Recovering his watch and money he went toward the door. There was a notice on the bulletin board:

THE TEAM WILL REPORT AT SUITE 977 IN THE

HOTEL CLEVELAND TONIGHT AT SIX THIRTY. THIS MEANS THE WHOLE SQUAD.

A bawling-out. Dave was going to tell them off for their playing. Well, they certainly had it coming.

6

The big bus with the words BROOKLYN BASE-
BALL CLUB over the driver in front drew up
at the hotel. A small crowd immediately col-
lected on the sidewalk, making an open path
through which the players had to pass into the
lobby. It was a home-town crowd and therefore
apathetic because they were waiting for their
heroes, the Indians. The Kid heard one or two
remark in disappointed tones, "It's only the
Dodgers." A few picked out Razzle, conspicu-
ously elegant in his green suit, and big Babe
Stansworth with his thumb bound up in plaster
and tape.

The lobby was jammed as usual. He went to the newsstand, bought several papers, and took the elevator to his room, listening to the comments in the crowded car. "Yeah, they're all washed up now." "The National League never was a first class league, not since . . . " "Why, Leonard had horseshoes to win the pennant with that bunch of boys." He stopped at his floor, glad to escape. Harry Street with whom he roomed on the road was already there counting his laundry.

"Nuts! They didn't send back my blue shirt." He picked up the telephone. "Hey there, sweetmeat, gimme room service."

Tired, discouraged, the Kid sat on the edge of the bed and kicked off his shoes. When a team lost it sure made a man feel tired. You were tired all right when you won, but not the same way. No, not the same way. He picked up the Series program which happened to be on the night stand beside the bed. Leaning back, he arranged the pillow and thumbed over the pages. How old was that bird Miller, anyhow? He came to his own photograph, and for the first time read the lines underneath the picture.

Roy (Kid) Tucker

Outfielder. A manager's dream. Great competitor, great fellow. Started back in 1939 as a pitcher with the Dodgers, hurt his arm, and like Johnny Cooney of the Braves made himself into an outfielder. Was a substitute last season until Tommy Scudder was traded to the Phillies for Elmer McCaffrey. Bats left. Throws right. Unmarried. Lives in Tomkinsville, Connecticut. Nickname: Bad News.

He threw the program on the floor. He hadn't been bad news for anyone save poor old Dave. Things looked tough for Dave unless they could pick up another game. Even so, MacManus would not likely bring him back the next season. MacManus had no use for losers. He strung along with winners. If only they could get another game. That was the reason for their meeting tonight; a good stiff fight talk and a change in the batting order. Maybe Dave would have to yank him from the line-up. He glanced at one of the newspapers full of pictures of the Cleveland players scoring runs, making catches in the field, running wild on the bases. Underneath he read the captions. Then he turned to Grantland Rice's column.

"Good pitching will always beat good hitting, and the Indians have the pitchers." Shoot, we haven't been hitting. We haven't hit like we can hit.

Another writer compared the two managers. Interested, the Kid looked over his remarks about Dave Leonard. "Leonard's secret of success in running the Dodgers this season has been in not over-managing. He has a club composed mainly of former players with whom he buddied as a player. He understands that too much bossing would be resented. So he ups with a system that gives his men latitude without too much rein. This has developed initiative to a greater degree than any other major league club."

"Here! Get a load of this." Harry, sitting on the side of his bed, unfolded a newspaper. "Casey says, he says . . . here . . . about Lanahan. Lanahan plays ground balls now like a member of the married men's team in an office field day. Ha, ha." Casey could invariably be depended upon for a chuckle. He was always funny. About the other team, anyway. The telephone rang.

"I hope they located my blue shirt. I like that blue shirt." Harry picked up the receiver. His newspaper fell to the bed and the Kid, leaning over, picked it up. He looked at Casey's column.

"It's the old pitch-punch show. As always, good pitching has the call. But the fact is the Dodgers are paralyzed. For the first time they're up against something new; American League fast-ball pitching. Moreover, they're dead on their feet. While the Indians coasted in to the pennant through September, the Dodgers had to fight right down to the last day of the season to outscuffle the Giants. The Dodger pitching staff is worn and weary. The Gowanus Gang is washed up."

He felt his face redden. That wasn't funny. It wasn't funny at all. Washed up! We are, are we? He read along. "The Dodgers one-two punch, with Babe Stansworth out, has failed miserably. Swanson has been a soft touch for all the Cleveland hurlers. Tucker is probably in worse shape from his beaning than anyone suspects. He gets dizzy out there in the sun and finds it difficult at times to hear out of his right ear."

Yes, there it was! ". . . and finds it difficult to hear out of his right ear."

"Hey, Harry! Just listen to this. Casey says I can't hear out of my right ear. Where does he get that stuff?"

"Aw, that bird! Last May he said I was sick with the flu and wouldn't be back in the line-up for two weeks. Gee, was I mad! My mother sent me the clipping from home. That same day I'd written her saying I was feeling fine and everything was dandy. She thought it was a lie and came hustling down to Chicago to find out. I like to paste Casey when I seen him in the dugout before the game that day."

"Yeah, but saying I'm deaf in one ear. And suppose the Dodgers let me out? Suppose I get that pink slip one of these days? What then? What chance have I got with any other club? Who wants a deaf mute around? Say, who do you guess told him that?"

"Nobody. He just made it up."

"Made it up?"

"Why, sure. He's too busy playing poker and gobbling his laughing soup at night to chase round and check on all the rumors floating about."

The Kid shook his head. He was sore and no

mistake. Leaning back, he shook the paper and read on.

"In the eighth this afternoon Andy Painter drove a deep one to right center. It was a hard hit ball but the Tucker of the days before he crashed into the Polo Ground wall would have been up against the fence and speared it. Those catches were a dime a dozen for the Dodger right fielder in the old days. But since that injury and since he was skulled by Gene Miller, the Kid from Tomkinsville is wall-shy. The ball got away for a double and a run. The fact is that Tuck is wall-shy and plate-shy, too. Leonard better write him off as a total loss."

There was lots more but he didn't care to go on. Instead he threw down the paper and jumped from the bed, his face flushed. Harry was busy telephoning. Harry was always telephoning. In every city of the circuit he spent his time telephoning. But say, that man Casey. . . wall-shy and plate-shy, was he? And deaf in one ear!

It wasn't true. Nosir, it wasn't true, none of it. "Look, Harry, look at what that fella says. . . ."

•

Occasionally someone in the club was late. Occasionally there were the usual stragglers filing in to a meeting or getting to a train gate after everyone had arrived. Not tonight. They all knew they were in for a lacing and nobody felt like making it worse by showing up late. Even Razzle in his green suit was solemn and subdued as Roy and Harry met him before the elevator. Together they got off and walked silently down the hall. At 977 they paused, picturing the scene inside. There would be Dave astride a chair, a toothpick waggling from one side of his mouth to the other, his face grim and serious. There would be the coaches near him, and opposite the circle of chairs, everyone wide-eyed and sober. So the three stood outside, hesitating. None of them wanted to knock.

"Come in." The door opened. There was no meeting. Instead a long table almost filled the room. Big bunches of flowers decorated the table and there were printed menu cards at each place. Already the small space around the long table was jammed. Laughter rose, and big Bill Hanson the business manager was pointing across to Karl Case. Dave stood by the door holding it open.

"Come in, boys, come in. Come in, Raz; come in, Roy. Hullo, Harry."

Never would the Kid forget that dinner. There

was no baseball. Baseball was out. No one talked baseball or mentioned the Series or the game that day. No one spoke of Gene Miller. Instead they were laughing at Charlie Draper giving an imitation of Babe Stansworth behind the plate, or smiling while Cassidy, the first base coach, exchanged wisecracks with Razzle and Harry Street. There was beer, plenty, in pitchers. Before long the whole room was noisy and happy. Everyone was at ease. But the thing they would never forget beside the atmosphere was the food.

It wasn't the regular food, the food they ate every day in the Coffee Shoppe. As Fat Stuff once remarked, that Coffee Shoppe food was cooked about three in the afternoon and kept warm in an oven until dinner time. This was real food, especially ordered for them. They started with a planked lake shad. The Kid had never eaten a planked shad before. It was wonderful. Then a steak and fried potatoes. Boy, what a steak! Even Charlie Draper who knew where to get the best meals all over the country said it was a good steak.

"Yeah, that's a good steak all right. That's a good steak, couldn't do better in Kansas City."

"But that's a K. C. steak right there, you bum." The boys laughed to see Charlie fooled.

Then a peach melba. Peach ice cream and crushed peaches and whipped cream, lots of it, poured over it. As much beer as you wanted, waiters filling up your glass from behind. The Kid preferred his favorite drink, a lime Coke.

Over everything was the noise and laughter, Raz's voice, and a spirit of comradeship. He felt himself one of the gang, warm and happy. It made him forget Casey and those smarting words.

"Babe, how much you weigh?" asked Raz.

Babe Stansworth at the end of the table looked up suspiciously. Too often he had been the butt of Razzle's jokes.

"What's it to you?"

"No kidding. What's your playing weight?"

"Two thirty."

"Two thirty. Two hundred thirty pounds, he weighs. Get that, fellas. Weighs two hundred and thirty and sits with a crossword puzzle in our room for half an hour trying to think up a three letter word for obese." The crowd roared.

"Fat Stuff would get that right off, wouldn't you, Fat Stuff?" The old pitcher looked up and grinned. He was deep in his steak, saying little.

"Hey, Elmer, how 'bout that jane you had the date with the other night? Did she show up?"

"Yeah, she showed up all right," said Red Allen, McCaffrey's roommate. "She showed up and you know where Elmer took her?"

"To the Ritz, I suppose," said Raz.

"Naw. He took her for a bus ride."

"Know what he says to her?" Bill Hanson's blue eyes shone. "He says, 'Sister, you know you got great potentialities.' And she says, 'Shhh . . . the driver'll hear you.' "

Laughter. More laughter. Dave's voice, quiet and relaxed, came down the table.

"Hank Butler? Yes, he was with me back in nineteen and thirty-one, you remember, Charlie. . . ." Time flew. Cigarettes were passed and cigars. Razzle stuck one in his mouth at the usual jaunty angle. Finally Dave rose. A kind of suspense hung over the room. Was it coming now? Was the dinner a prelude to a grim scene, was baseball coming back? Then he spoke.

"All right, boys. Everyone had enough? You, there, Rats . . . sure you finished?" Rats Doyle ate twice as fast and twice as much as anyone on the club. "If you're ready, Rats, we'll move on."

"Aw, leave him here. Cassidy didn't finish all his steak."

"Okay, Rats? Everyone set? We're going to a burlesque show. Century Theatre, corner Grand and Cuyahoga. Bill Hanson has the tickets. Bill will give each man his ticket. It's nearly eight now and time to go. Everyone ready? Get your seat from Hanson and let's get going."

After the show they walked along in a bunch to the hotel. A few stepped into a kind of open store with a rifle range at the rear. Dave stood watching. "Why, Roy," he said, "I hadn't any idea you were such a good shot."

"Yessir . . . yes, Dave. We do quite a bit of shooting on the farm every fall. Until I went to work in town we did."

"What you shoot up there on that farm, Kid? Lions?"

Roy flushed. "Yeah, lions . . . and tigers. And sometimes Indians, too, Razzle."

Raz, to whom the word Indian was not exactly a subject for jesting, quit like most jesters when he found himself on the receiving end. They reached the hotel and went into the crowded lobby over which hung an air of excitement. In his green suit, green hat, green shirt and neck-

tie, Razzle was instantly picked out and surrounded by autograph hunters.

"They say Dempsey signs over five hundred
autographs a day," said Charlie Draper at the
Kid's side. "Hullo . . . there's Connie Mack
over there."

"Where? Where? Which one?" Connie was a
hero of Roy's.

"Over there against that pillar. Wanna meet
him?"

"I sure do."

They picked their way through the groups of
talking, gesticulating men. Draper touched him
on the shoulder. He looked around with a quick,
youthful movement. Tall, thin, an erect carriage,
deep blue eyes, he acted and looked far less
than his almost eighty years.

"Hullo, Mr. Mack." The old fellow's face lit
up with a warm glow.

"Why, Charlie! Charlie Draper!" He pro-
nounced the words precisely, with emphasis.
"How are you? I'm glad to see you. How you
making it?"

"Pretty good, Mr. Mack. Say, I'd like you to
meet Roy Tucker, our right fielder."

His hand was firm and strong. "Yes, sir, I'm
real glad to meet you."

"Glad to meet you, Mr. Mack." The Kid wanted to say more, to tell him that ever since the great days of Grove, Cochrane, Simmons, and Earnshaw he had been his hero, although he had never dreamed of meeting him.

"Yes, yes. Been watching you out there. You keep on, son, and you're gonna be a ballplayer. I was telling Dave the other day, Charlie, I'd be mighty pleased to have this boy on my club."

"Gee! Thanks, lots, Mr. Mack."

Charlie said something but the Kid lost his words in the loud tones which came from behind. The familiar voice of Harry Street, now rasping and harsh, drowned out Charlie's remark.

"Let me tell you something, Casey, you can't get away with that stuff round here. We know him too well."

"Aw, I say he's yeller. A yeller busher with a big head. Gets conked once and he's all washed up."

The Kid whirled about. Casey and Harry had their chins together in anger. He pushed his roommate out of the way. "What's that you were saying, Casey?"

"I said you were washed up."

"I heard you. And you said something else, too. Better take it back. In a hurry."

"Or you'll make me, hey? You and your six big brothers here."

The sneer was too much. It touched off his resentment of the afternoon, set his irritated nerves afire. Hardly realizing what he was doing, he felt his fist against Casey's round chin. The sportswriter staggered back, pulled himself together, and came on, his face angry and aflame.

Once more Roy caught him full on the jaw. The burly figure went down as someone grabbed the Kid.

"Get upstairs." It was Charlie Draper, his arms round him, shoving him toward the elevator. "Get upstairs quick. Lock your door and whatever you do don't answer the phone."

7

The meeting that next morning was short.

"Boys, there are two departments of play, batting and fielding. They should be separate in the minds of all you men, but they aren't. When a player isn't hitting, he takes his slump out there on the field. He broods about his inability to hit. His mind isn't concentrated on his fielding so he makes mistakes. He boots one. I never knew it to fail. Then he starts thinking about that error he made and takes it up to bat with him. So he doesn't hit. That's the way it goes.

"Now I want you should all forget what's happened. If you can forget you'll begin to hit. Once you begin to hit, everything will be fine. No club looks good when they're not hitting. I think we must have set a record of some sort these last three games for men left on bases. But we'll come out of it. We have power. If we're not a power team we're nothing. Try and get relaxed. That's the trouble with you, Roy, and you too, Swanny. I was watching you both at the plate yesterday. You each had your elbows too close to your sides; you were all tied up. Remember, those elbows have gotta be out from your body, and your bat well off your shoulder to get a free swing. Don't forget it, any of you."

Nothing yet about the Casey episode. Yet surely Dave had heard all about it by now. Nothing escaped that old fox. The Kid waited, wondering, as the manager, toothpick in his mouth, continued. "I know we can win. I got plenty of confidence in this here ball club. However, no use talking, the chips are down. We can't kid ourselves; we must pull this one out today. Rats, you'll pitch. Now that ball to McClusky, where was it? High inside? Yeah? But we said we'd pitch low to him. Didn't we? Didn't we agree?" He looked around. Solemn nods. Yes, they'd agreed on that.

"All right. Rats, I want you should pitch to Hammy and Lanahan like I told you. Lanahan's been hitting us hard. Catfish Crawford came up to the room late last night and said we oughta pitch low to him all the time. Whaddya say we crowd Painter?"

"Le's pitch over his fist to Lanahan. He can't hurt us more'n he has."

"Okay, we'll do that. And we'll throw McClusky some slow balls. We haven't slowed up to him in the whole Series yet. If Spike Johnson goes in today, don't forget he's got a mighty mean sinker. Let's not give them a chance to get going. Soon's he throws you one you can hit, sock it. All we need is two-three runs. Whatever you do, don't worry. Keep relaxed. The ability to relax is what makes a money player in every sport, boys. Remember, we've come from behind lots of times this season, and if you'll play the game you're capable of playing, the game I know you can play, we'll come from behind again. That licking we took yesterday doesn't mean a thing. Not one thing. All right . . . any questions . . . anyone . . .

"Yesterday I met up with Joe Jacobson, old friend of mine, now manager in Tulsa. Joe's up for the Series, and I met him in the lobby as we came in. Joe started to ride me. 'What you-all gonna do with those tickets you been printing for that game in Brooklyn tomorrow?' he asks me.

" 'We're gonna sell 'em,' I told him." There was a ring of determination in his voice. "Okay. Let's go."

And there was a ring of determination in the sound of their spikes; clack-clack, clackety-clack, clack-clack on the concrete. They were going to win. They were determined to win for Dave. No one more so than the Kid. Dave hadn't said a word about Casey. That was the kind of a guy he was. He knew who was right in that little incident, Dave did.

After some batting practice, with no Casey visible among the mob of sportswriters on the field and climbing over them in the dugout, Roy walked out to his place in right field to chase fungoes. The fans were there in the cheap bleacher seats, attentive, watching, knowledgeable. To be sure they were not his own fans, but they were fans, with a fan's sense of humor as he soon found out.

"Hey, Kid," someone called affectionately from the bleachers when he came near them. He waved his hand. Instantly the reply came back.

"You big bum!" Not the Brooklyn retort, but

close enough to make him think he was at home again.

The game began. Rats lasted exactly two innings. The Cleveland powerhouse went to work in the second. A single, another single, and a double. Two runs across and McClusky dancing confidently off second. From his place the Kid watched Rats dejectedly stuff his glove into his pocket and take the longest walk in the world—the walk to the showers. In the stands the wolves rose jeering, while from the Indian dugout noise and chatter resounded. It was in the bag. Three games to one. Two runs to the good. Yep, a tough spot for the Dodgers.

Doggone, thought Roy, I won't quit. I won't stop fighting. Why, we're better than that. I just know we are. We haven't showed it, but we are. Now who'll Dave throw in? Elmer? Or maybe take a chance on Raz? Nosir. It's old Fat Stuff.

Yes, there was Fat Stuff in the bullpen, pretending as usual he didn't hear, and burning in a few more practice throws. Old Fat Stuff, the reliable. He waddled across the field, a barrel-chested figure, long arms swinging by his side. And who's that . . . it can't be . . . it is! Dave! Dave going in to catch him!

Gosh! Dave was back at the plate. Dave was

in there. The old battery, Foster and Leonard. Now we'll go places. Now you just watch our dust.

Dave strapped on the breast protector, took Foster's throw, and rifled the ball to Ed at second base, while shouts from every part of the field in confident tones showed how the team felt.

"All right, Dave."

"Atta boy, Dave old kid, old boy . . . "

"Right behind you, Dave."

"Le's go, Dave . . . "

Dave back! Gee, it was great to have him there. Fat Stuff threw his last warm-up pitch as the applause sprinkled through the Cleveland stands. Foster and Leonard. Why, they were together on the old White Sox back in 1934. They'd forgotten, the two of them, more baseball than the Indians ever knew.

The first man hit a pop foul. "Yours, Dave . . . yours . . . Dave . . . Dave . . . Dave." The cries had the same confidence in them. West might stumble over a bat; even Babe Stansworth could trip on his mask or muff a pop-up. Not Dave. Not old Surefoot. "Atta boy, Dave, good catch, old timer." You could always depend on Dave in the clutch.

Hammy, the Indian slugger, came to the plate. From his position in right the Kid could see the two veterans go to work on him. Fat Stuff wasted his first ball. Then he got a strike, low, then a called strike. He took the signal and wound up. Hammy caught it and slammed it back. The ball traveled like a bullet, catching Fat Stuff just below the belt. He went down as if he'd been shot. But the fighting instinct which was part of the pitcher's make-up woke him long enough to get the ball across to first. Running in to back up, the Kid saw Fat Stuff collapse, saw the throw nip the runner at first, and as everyone's eyes were on the stricken pitcher he saw McClusky, running wild, dash for the plate.

"Home . . . Red . . . home . . . quick . . . home."

The big first baseman heard his voice and shot the ball to Dave Leonard, crouching and ready at the plate in time to nab McClusky. A double-play and the inning was over.

Meanwhile the Dodgers formed a circle around Fat Stuff. Just as they were getting ready to carry him off, he came to.

"Wait a sec . . . if I can only sit still a few minutes, I'll be all right."

So they assisted him to the bench where he sat as long as he could, which wasn't long because he was the second batter. Dave, the first man up, had drawn a base on balls.

The stands applauded when the big man with his bat toddled to the plate. Not a bad hitter, and like most pitchers proud of his hitting, he stood balancing his club. In the box Spike Johnson nodded to his catcher and wound up. The ball came close, the batter turned, turned . . . and caught it full on the ribs. For the second time in ten minutes he fell, groggy, to the ground.

The Dodger bench jumped to their feet with a roar of rage. This was too much! First the Kid, now Fat Stuff! Swanson rushed at Johnson who was hurrying in. He swung first, missed Swanny, and the Dodger caught him full on the nose. McCormick, the Cleveland catcher, mask off jumped on Swanny. Karl Case ran up and swung on McCormick. The catcher went down on his back, heels in the air.

In five seconds there was a terrific melee at the plate. Fists and spikes flying, a mix-up of players writhed on the ground while poor old Fat Stuff, entirely neglected, rolled on the grass, trying to catch his breath. When the players were finally separated and order restored, the game continued with patched up teams on both sides. Johnson and McCormick were banished. So were Swanny and Case. With two of their best hitters out, with an injured pitcher in the box and a forty-year-old catcher behind the plate, the Dodgers went after that two run lead.

Red Allen hit into a doubleplay, chiefly because Fat Stuff was a slow runner. Now there were two men out with Dave on third. The Kid came to the plate against Paul Drewes, Cleveland's relief pitcher. If only he could hit that ball. If only he could hit. He was still in a daze after his scrap with Casey. Shaking his head, he tried to forget it, to concentrate on the pitcher. The ball came and he swung. But by the sound he knew it was no good. Just a Baltimore chop that struck in front of the plate. Another easy out at first.

Don't carry it with you into the field. Forget it. Forget Casey. And the batting slump. And the situation. Dave was back, wasn't he? Now they'd pull out. They'd go ahead.

Yet inning after inning went by with no runs scored, and the figure 2 on the scoreboard looked as big as a million. Pale, lame, and sore, Fat Stuff in the box hung on by sheer will power, aided by Dave's knowledge of the hitters.

In the last of the seventh Bruce Gordon, a dangerous man, came to the plate with two men out. Dave waved the Kid toward the right. Still in a kind of daze, he obeyed slowly and was moving just as Gordon caught the pitch and smacked a tremendous drive his way. The wind caught the ball and carried it foul. Had he been on his toes as he should have been it would have meant an easy out.

Just the same, try. You never know. Try, run, run. There . . . it was falling . . . almost. Through the roar of the crowd he heard Red Allen warning him. "Watch it . . . Roy . . . watch the stand . . . watch it . . ." Hang it all, he had to get that ball. Wall-shy, was he? They'd see whether he was wall-shy.

From the stands in right field the crowd watched. Too bad, an impossible catch. No, he's after it! They rose as he strained forward to the bleachers, desperately reaching for the ball, closer, closer. Look out, he'll hit the wall. With a final burst of speed he stuck up one hand, caught it, and stumbling rolled over on the turf right against the barrier. At last he picked himself up, the ball safe in his glove.

There! How do you like that, Casey? Wall-shy, am I? Yeah! The best one hand of anybody in the business, that's what they said last year. Listen to 'em yell. Say, the fans in this man's town are fair after all, aren't they? Three out. "All right, gimme my bat, boy. Give us that heavy stick there. Who's up, Allen? I'm next. We gotta have a rally. Give us a start, big boy, I'll bring you round. Wait and see if I don't."

"Roy, step up there and get me a hit. You're better'n you've shown so far. Go get me a single. There goes Red!"

Red Allen was fast. But fast as he was, old Lanahan's arm was faster. The runner almost beat the throw, but the ball was there ahead of him. No! Hammy dropped it. He dropped it! The coaches danced with delight on the base paths. Here's where we go. Man on first and nobody out. The Kid grabbed the heavy bat. I can always hit better with men on bases, he thought. That was a slow ball Drewes threw Red, I noted particular. Hope he throws me a slow ball, I can hit 'em.

It *was* a slow ball and he caught it squarely. All he saw was old Cassidy urging him along from first, Lanahan dancing near second yet keeping well out of the path of his flying spikes, and then Charlie Draper back of third giving him the slide signal. The ball was still in the air as he felt the gorgeous touch of the canvas sack at his feet.

Now the Dodger dugout was alive with pepper and noise. For the first time since the first game they had a chance really to yell. Sitting on the step they shouted at him through cupped hands. Swanny's substitute flied out, and for a moment they cooled down, but then Whitehouse, substituting for Karl Case, came up. He looked at the outfielders, surveyed the situation, knocked the dirt from his spikes. The pitcher wound up.

Another hit! McClusky and Gordon were both scampering after it. Once the ball landed, the Kid danced into the plate and stood watching McClusky reach it, fumble it momentarily, and then drop it. Finally he grabbed it and threw to Gordon, while Whitehouse, a jackrabbit on bases, was scooting round third and tearing for home. Turning to throw, Gordon slipped, caught himself, and burned the ball in hurriedly. The throw was wide and in a flurry of dust Whitehouse came across the plate with their third run.

They scored another, and somehow Fat Stuff hung on. He weakened toward the end, but sheer heart carried him through, for the only way he would go off the field was on a stretcher.

In a short while the game was over. Clack-clack, clackety-clack, clack-clack their spikes sounded gaily on the concrete runway. Crunch-crunch, crunch-crunch their spikes beat a joyful tune as they poured onto the wooden floor of the dressing room. Laughing, yelling, shouting, they threw themselves down.

"Swell playing, Roy. . . ."

"Great work, Roy. . . ."

"Thanks, Karl . . . thanks, Harry. . . ."

"Nice going out there, Fat Stuff. . . ."

"Meat and potatoes, oh, boy. . . ."

"Nice hitting, Whitey. . . ."

"Thanks, Chisel . . . how's for a Coke? . . . "

"Whoopee . . . yippee. . . ."

Yells, shouts, confusion. They sat shaking their fists at each other in triumph across the room. "I knew you could do it, Roy. Boy, did you bust that ball."

"Yowser. Fellas, that's one game we really wanted, I'm telling you all."

"Great work, Fat Stuff. Great going out there."

"Thanks, Harry, thanks, Roy. . . ."

For a while they sat, exultant and perspiring, reading their fan mail and telegrams, too content to move, drinking Cokes and calling across the room to each other.

Now the photographers crowded in. The photographers had left them alone since their victory in the first game. Now they stood on tables, benches, chairs. They shot Fat Stuff shaking hands with Dave. They took Red in every conceivable pose. They came sparking their flashlights right in your face. Inside the manager's room Dave was soon surrounded by sportswriters. The Dodgers were still in the race.

In the main room there was a large square wooden box in front of each locker which the players were filling up with clean clothes. These boxes would be emptied and put into the equipment trunks to go by express direct to Brooklyn. Their wet, dirty clothes they handed to Chisel to dry out before being packed. Old Chisel walked among them, happy and radiant as the others. Yessir, the Dodgers were still in the running.

"Don't forget your jackets, boys. Paper says it may be cold back home. A cold spell is coming. Don't forget your bats neither."

In an undershirt and no trousers Dave came through the room to the table in the middle piled with telegrams and letters. He looked them over, attacked the while by half a dozen reporters who stood at his elbow bombarding him with question after question. Casey, the Kid observed, was not among them. Then he noticed MacManus come in, pleased and grinning from ear to ear. The crinkles were deep about his blue eyes as he went round the room, patting Fat Stuff on the back, shaking hands with Harry; congratulating everyone. For Dave in the center he paused with a word but nothing more. The Kid watched with disappointment as the Irishman passed along and came to his locker.

"Nice going, Roy. You sure came through for us this afternoon." He turned away as Sandy Martin of the *Post* caught his arm and asked him a question.

"It wasn't me, Mr. MacManus, or Fat Stuff; it was Dave who pulled us through. We were doing it for Dave; we were in there scrapping with him, for him." That was what the Kid longed to say to MacManus. But the moment vanished.

"Holy suffering swordfish, Sandy, how do I know who'll pitch tomorrow. Why doncha ask Leonard?"

Slowly the Kid stripped and went into the showers, now filled with a joyous, yelling mob.

"Yippee, yowser . . . well, we sure got to that boy Drewes."

"Nice pitching, Fat Stuff, nice pitching."

"Nice pitching, hell! Did you see that single I laced out?"

"Good going out there, Roy. Nice runing on that catch."

"Yep, nice running, Kid. You started things out there."

"I started nothing. Red started them." He wasn't anxious to talk about that catch. He hated to admit he had been asleep in the field. Dave would know. Dave missed nothing no matter where he was, behind the plate or in the dugout. Dave would have seen.

He rubbed himself dry. Gosh, but it was swell to be on the winning side once more. It was great to be winning at last. Who said they couldn't hit? And who said he was plate-shy; yes, and wall-shy, too? He felt fresh and keen, ready to go out there and play nine innings. So, apparently, did everyone else. The room was noisy with laughter and shouts, crowded with sportswriters, photographers, radio men, old players, friends of the coaches. The Kid paused for a moment as he went past the bulletin board.

BROOKLYN BASEBALL CLUB

Next city: New York. Train leaves Union

tion at 6:15 P.M. Via Buffalo, Albany.
Arrives New York, 9:35 A.M. Baggage ready
at 5:15 P.M.

8

The siren screeched. It screeched again and again over the busy downtown streets of Cleveland while the team sat back, relaxed and happy, in the bus. A police escort from the Stadium to the station. They sure did things right for you in this town. And tomorrow was another day.

There were more police waiting on the sidewalk when they alighted, and they had made a line through the mob into the station. With quick steps the squad filed through. A scattering of applause greeted them and there were comments from the crowd on each side. These comments were different in tone and texture from the disparaging remarks they had heard on returning beaten to the hotel the previous afternoon.

"There's Razzle Nugent. Hi there, Raz. . . ."

"Where's Leonard . . . there he is . . . see . . . in front. . . ."

"And Swanson. And Roy Tucker. And Stansworth, the big guy in the brown hat with his thumb done up."

"Which one is Tucker? Which one?"

They came to the train gate. On the big signboard was a notice in large, white letters: BROOKLYN AND CLEVELAND BASEBALL CLUBS. RESERVED FOR PLAYERS ONLY.

At the gate stood Bill Hanson, the business manager, checking them off. "Case . . . Fat Stuff . . . Raz . . . where's Razzle . . . anyone seen Razzle?"

"He's gone to get some newspapers."

"They're on the train. Tell him to hurry up; we leave right away. Swanson . . . Tucker . . . Allen . . . Roth . . . West . . ."

The Kid passed through and down to the tracks and the train. The Cleveland team was already aboard. They had the rear end of the train with a diner, while the Dodgers had the front end and a diner of their own. Finding their baggage, the gang settled down. Outside on the platform a few curious faces of trainmen and conductors peered up at them, trying to pick out the players in their civilian clothes. Raz's elegant green suit flashed past, and he burst into the car to be greeted by cheers, for they were in a mood to yell at anything. In several minutes the conductor below waved his hand and swung aboard the step. The car shook slightly and started to glide from the station. They were off! On the last journey of the year.

Food. That was their first thought as soon as the train started and they knew, according to custom, that the diner would be open. They had all eaten at nine that morning and were hungry. Winning made them more hungry. In a mass they descended upon the diner directly ahead. Perspiring waiters were soon rushing back and forth through the swaying car with heavy trays of food. There was a silence save for the clatter of knives and forks. Everyone attended to the business of eating and even Razzle was silent for a while. The Kid glanced around. The last time the team would eat together as a team, he thought. Was it the last time they would eat with Dave?

After dinner they returned to their car and set-

tled down. Razzle began to leaf over the pages of
Time. Several players started the inevitable
game of rummy. A few read newspapers. Most
were talking, contented and relaxed. Only
Swanson, Case, and Jerry Strong, always serious, were discussing the problem of the hour—
Gene Miller. They knew they'd have to face him
again to win the Series.

Swanny, who hadn't got a single hit off
Miller, shook his head. "What did you do that
first game, Karl? Shorten your stride, or
what?"

Like most ballplayers, Karl wasn't sure what
he had done. "Well," continued Swanny, "you
hit him all over the lot in that first game, and I
haven't been able to get a loud foul offa him."

From the end of the car came Raz's voice over
his magazine. "Hey . . . Harry . . . hey,
Street . . . d'ja see Sue come in there this afternoon? All draped up in furs and everything?"

Someone else spoke. "I tell ya, we'll win! If we
don't grab this Series I'll eat my hat."

From across the aisle came the retort, "Aw,
you don't wear a hat."

"Then I'll eat yours. No, tell you what, I'll eat
Razzle's." Raz's green hat to match his suit was
the secret envy of the majority. Only Raz would

dare to wear such a costume and such colors. A chorus of approval up and down the aisle greeted this remark.

"Know how I knew we was in the Series? Know how I knew long before the end?" It was Red Allen from the seat behind. "My uncle Hank in Red Falls, Minnesota, ain't heard from him for eight years, writes and asks can I get him six seats for the three games in Cleveland. Good seats, please, he says."

"Yeah, they don't realize we all have to pay. I paid about sixty bucks for seats for my folks."

"Sure. Everyone pays. Except Judge Landis."

"Landis pays. Same as I do. Same as Dave, or MacManus."

". . . And when I give the seats to my missis, I say, 'Listen, kid, if you go to a ball game, just give your ears a chance.'"

Big Babe Stansworth looked up from his crossword puzzle. "Me too. So do I, Red. Say, what's a six letter word meaning late for dinner?"

Across the aisle sat Fat Stuff, laboriously writing with the stub of a pencil in his notebook. His notebook was famous all over the League. Every time the old pitcher threw to a new man, he summed up the batter's strength and weakness in his tattered notebook. His observations from the bench were also there. That, the Kid realized, was why Fat Stuff was still one of the smartest pitchers in the business in spite of his age. He watched him carefully copying down notes made on the field.

"Hey, Fat Stuff! D'you mind if I look at your notebook?"

The old pitcher looked up at the rookie, pleased. "No. 'Course not. C'mon over."

Roy slid into the seat beside the veteran. "Thanks, lots. I might just learn something." He watched while the veteran went over each Cleveland hitter: Lanahan, Hammerstein, Painter, Gordon, McClusky. There was a series of strange signs after each one. Fat Stuff explained them all: weak on high inside; left-handed pull hitter, hits to left field; straightaway hitter, steps into ball; right-handed, dumps toward third; dangerous bunter. He hadn't been watching from the bench through the Series for nothing. When he stepped out there to pitch he had each man diagnosed and knew how to work on them. Under each batter's name he had one written line.

"Don't walk him."

Fat Stuff closed the book, put an elastic round

it, and slipped this precious possession into his pocket. He carried it everywhere, even on the field, and some of the boys said that his roommate declared he put it in his pajamas at night, too.

"Gotta see Leonard," he announced briefly.

The Kid slipped back into his seat. Outside it was dark. The train slowed down, rumbled through a small Ohio town, movie theaters a-glitter, the main street crowded with people and parked cars. Why, sure, it was Saturday night. Funny how you lose track of the days on a ball club.

He picked up a newspaper. It was opened at Casey's column. No one had mentioned the fight of the night before and Casey had not been visible all afternoon. For a moment he wondered whether he would read what the sportswriter said or not. He didn't want to, yet something forced him. Here goes . . .

"The rules of baseball require each team to have a catcher in the field. With the failure of Hank West, rookie backstop, to come through after Babe Stansworth's injury put him out of the Series, radical measures were necessary. So something radical was done. Forty-year-old Dave Leonard, the Dodger manager, braving entanglement with his long gray whiskers, stepped behind the plate in the fifth game of the Series today. . . ."

Someone tapped him on the shoulder. "Hey! Leonard wants to see you. He's in Compartment D, next to the diner." It was Fat Stuff.

For a moment the Kid sat still. The newspaper rustled to the floor. There was something ominous in those words. Dave wanted to see him. It could only be about one thing. Well, Dave was a square shooter. He'd see things from the player's point of view.

He walked through the swaying diner where in clouds of smoke MacManus with Charlie Draper and two men he didn't know sat over drinks. He reached the next car. It had a corridor running down one side and doors opening off the corridor. There was a heavy carpet on the floor, and the corridor was painted a faint green color. Flossy, he thought. Several doors were open showing luxurious compartments. Cassidy sat in one, his shoes off, his feet on the opposite seat, smoking and looking out of the window. From another came laughter and the sound of voices as he passed. He looked at the letters on the doors.

"I had a king and two queens to start . . ."

"No, he didn't call me either. He stayed, that's all."

Here it was, D. He knocked. Dave was alone, his coat off, working over a mass of papers on a table. He rose and shut the door.

"Hullo there, Roy! Come in, come in. Take a seat, boy." There was the same warmth and friendliness in his voice as ever; also concern. He came to the point. No asking useless questions, no preliminaries.

"Roy, what's this I hear about your socking Casey in the lobby of the Cleveland last night?"

"That's correct, Dave."

He shook his head and looked out the window. Reaching into his vest pocket he pulled out a toothpick. That means trouble, thought the Kid. He knew the manager's ways.

"But, Roy, that's pretty serious. You must realize we can't have players on this club who go round socking sportswriters. Where'd we be?"

Dave didn't understand the whole story. Dave just hadn't heard it all. Dave was a fair guy. He'd better explain to Dave. "You see, Dave, it's like this. Casey has been riding me for some time now. Other day he lit into me, used most of his column to say I was wall-shy and plate-shy and Heaven only knows what-all."

"I know, I read it. He's said just as bad about Razzle and most of the other boys. That's no excuse."

"Wait a sec, Dave. He said that the beaning had made me deaf in my right ear. Never checked, or anything, or even asked me. . . ."

"Yes, but they's always stories going round about everyone in a World Series. He probably heard the Doc say it might affect your right ear or something like that. You can't expect . . ."

"But, Dave, this is different. I might lose my job on account of that crack. I might never get another one."

"Sure, you might. Same with me or Razzle and the pitchers. I know men who've been hounded out of baseball for one reason or another by sportswriters. They don't handle you with gloves. That's no reason to go running round a hotel lobby socking . . ."

Distinctly this wasn't so good. It wasn't working out the way he'd expected. Dave was hard to convince. Dave had most likely heard the story from Casey. He went on.

"But you haven't heard the rest of it. Then came the pay-off. That night in the lobby . . . last night, it was." It seemed a hundred years back. "Casey was standing there talking to

Harry and said I was scared. Called me yellow. I heard him, Dave; I turned round and heard him say it."

"So you socked him on the chin."

"Uhuh. Most anyone would, with any guts."

"Not ballplayers, Roy."

"If they don't, they'd oughta . . . "

There was a moment's pause. "Well, Roy, if that's the way you feel about things, I really don't know that baseball can use you any more."

The train lurched round a corner. Awkwardly the Kid pulled himself back onto his seat. He was dazed, almost as if he'd been beaned. Dave didn't understand, didn't see his angle at all.

The toothpick waggled in the old catcher's face. It did a dance from one side of his mouth to the other. For a minute that was a year neither spoke. Then, looking away from him, eyes on the lights of a small town flashing past the window, the manager continued.

"Roy, it's like this. Without publicity baseball would be dead. And you'd be back on that farm, Roy, and Heaven only knows where I'd be. That publicity comes from the newspapers. Or rather it comes through the sportswriters the newspapers send out. Why do you suppose the ball clubs pay the expenses of those reporters in the training camps down South? Even take their families along, too. The publicity, Roy. That's what makes baseball.

"Now I'm not saying you haven't had some provocation, that you didn't have cause to sock him. So have I and Swanny and almost every ballplayer who ever got anywhere. Point is you forget one thing. For every knock there's a boost. Have you forgotten last year and that roughhouse in the Schenley in Pittsburgh, when Raz came in and found you reading Casey's column telling what a great man you were? Remember?"

Gosh, Dave was wonderful. How did he know that at the precise moment Razzle had broken down the door of his room he had been reading Casey's column? He remembered the scene, the insistent knocking, the words of the sportswriter even. ". . . he'll take advice, and the boys say he'll get better as he goes along . . . several games he's won by timely hits . . . he's as fast as anyone on the club, he can throw, and if he could cook I'd marry him."

The manager continued. "Now, Roy, this might have had serious consequences. If Judge Landis had got hold of it, there'd have been an investigation and you'd been suspended. The

Dodgers going into the last two games without their right fielder and one of their best hitters!" Say, that was serious. He didn't realize, he'd hardly appreciated . . .

"Roy, club owners won't permit ballplayers to go round socking newspapermen on the puss. You . . . I don't say, mind you, that you didn't have provocation. But I recall MacManus warned you about Casey before the third game. He told you that chap always likes to be riding someone. It's lucky most of the other sportswriters don't like him, so they hushed the thing up and it got no further."

Yes, he'd been wrong. Unquestionably he'd been wrong. He should have kept his temper. He oughtn't to have slugged Casey. That was bad, all right.

"There's only one thing to do. Two things to do. First, Roy, I've got to fine you a hundred and fifty dollars. I sure hate to do it. But I must. MacManus would fire me in a minute if I didn't, and he'd be quite justified. It hurts, Roy, to have to set you down like this, because you're one player on this club that never caused me a moment's trouble. Not a moment, ever since you joined us down there in Clearwater in the spring of '39. But . . . got to do it. The club owners just won't allow fights with sportswriters, and that's about all there is to it. Understand?"

He understood. He wasn't happy. He didn't like the situation. But he saw he had had a lucky escape. After all, as Dave said . . .

The manager went on, still looking intently out the window, apparently seeing something in the blackness.

"One more thing, Roy. You'll have to apologize to Casey."

"Me? Apologize? To Casey? Me . . . me apologize?" This was too much. The fine, yes. But apologizing?

"I'm afraid *so*."

"But Dave . . ." This rankled. This hurt. Why, he hadn't done anything but slug a guy. Lots of people did that. It was Casey who ought to apologize to him. Casey had called him yellow. He was bewildered and upset.

The old catcher leaned over and laid a hand on his leg. "Roy, it's like this. There's lots of injustices in life and lots in baseball, too, because baseball is part of life. We simply have to make the best of them, that's all. This is a tough situation for you and I'm sorry; but you got yourself in it and you'll have to get yourself out. Now go back there and try to go to sleep. You need it. Tomorrow likely you'll feel better about the whole thing. I know, it smarts right now; but tomorrow things will seem different. Don't let this get you down."

He stumbled back along the tinted green corridor. Hang it all, he hadn't done anything. It was Casey who had begun the scrap, who had called him yellow. It was all Casey's fault. The fine, yes, that was reasonable enough maybe, because he himself had lost his temper and slugged the sportswriter. But apologizing was different. He'd be darned if he would apologize.

To himself he kept saying this, through the diner and into his own car and while he was undressing. But as he buttoned the curtains and finally snapped off the light, he knew in the end he would.

9

Ready save for the last thing of all, lacing his shoes, the Kid sat on a four-legged stool beside his locker. That catch in foul territory and the three-bagger of the previous afternoon made him happier. Once again he felt he might get into his stride, might live up to his nickname. But the Casey business was tough. Sure enough, that was tough. Ever since he had turned over in bed and seen the October sunshine streaming in the window that morning, he had been saying to himself that he would never apologize. Nope, he wouldn't apologize. Yet all the time he knew he would.

Staring gloomily at the wooden floor, pockmarked by the scars of thousands of spikes, he listened to the shouts and laughter across the way. A hot game of cards was in progress, with three or four kibitzers watching. Dave was walking around, a word here, a word there, talking to this man, giving advice to another, listening to someone's comments on the Indian batters. But the Kid kept his gaze away from the old catcher. He didn't want to talk to him.

At last, however, Dave reached his locker, pulled up a stool, and sat down. The Kid felt that the mere mention of Casey's name would make him burst. There was none. Instead, the manager sat there saying nothing for a moment, with a ball in his hands. He passed the ball from one hand to the other.

"Roy . . . what did you hit against him yesterday? That three-bagger, I mean. A slow one by the letters? I thought so. You didn't hit it hard, either, but it sure traveled."

It sure did. Dave's confidence made him feel better. His resentment vanished. Eagerly he explained. "No, it wasn't a hard hit ball, really, just met squarely, that's all."

Dave nodded, listening. "Good. Go in there this afternoon and play for me like you did yes-

terday. That's all I ask." He rose, the ball under
one armpit, and clapped his hands together.

"All right now, boys."

The card game ceased. The players looked up
from their lockers and formed a circle round the
old catcher. Razzle came in from the washroom
where he had been putting ointment on his
black hair and slicking it down. Dave, a toothpick in his mouth, sat across a chair with his
arms as usual over the back. While he talked he
slapped the ball from one hand to the other.

"Well, boys, what say we go out there and grab
off this game? We're back on the old home
grounds at last, with our fans behind us, and
you all know what a difference that can make in
a tight place. This-here ballpark suits us much
better than that stadium in Cleveland. Some of
those hits that were caught there are going into
the stands here. If he pitches Thomas, don't
worry; he can't beat us this time. And don't take
anything off him. Go up there and hit him hard
whenever you get a good one.

"I feel this is in the bag. Those boys aren't
going to play so well here in Brooklyn. They got
something coming to 'em. Just go down the line
like we were talking the other day. Whatever
happens, don't tighten up. You were loose yes-

terday, especially toward the end of that game. I want you should stay that way, all of you."

He looked around the circle at his pitchers; at Raz with the slicked-down mane of hair, at old Fat Stuff, ready despite his shaking-up the day before to go out and throw to the hitters, at McCaffrey, a new man in the Series, at Rats and Speed Boy Davis and Rog Stinson, at all the men who had pitched the team into a pennant. Now the chips were down indeed. They had to have this game. Which one would he choose?

The ball went back and forth from one hand to the other. It was the only betrayal of nerves he showed. Then with a movement of his forearm he tossed the ball over to Elmer McCaffrey who caught it in his glove. McCaffrey pitching! The signal to break up.

Crunch-crunch, crunch-crunch, went their spikes on the wooden floor. They moved to the door. Clack-clack, clackety-clack, they sounded on the concrete outside on the stadium runway.

The field, and especially the part back of the diamond, was black with figures of cameramen, reporters, old ballplayers, autograph hunters, and others who had come early and managed to get out onto the grass. McCaffrey stood aside as the Kid stepped out on the playing surface.

Whenever he was pitching, the big boy always insisted on being the last man on the field. The Kid didn't smile at this. Everyone had superstitions. He himself never stepped on a foul line if he could help it. Bad luck! Raz refused to autograph a baseball unless he was in uniform. Swanny always touched second base on his way to take up his position in center field. Fat Stuff wore his sweat socks until they almost fell off. Lucky, they were, he said. Red, with two strikes on him, invariably pulled the gum from his mouth and put it on the button of his cap. Even Dave never failed to pull his left shoe on before his right one.

Then, walking toward the dugout, the Kid saw him. He was ahead, standing by the water cooler, talking to Swanny and Sandy Martin of the *Post* and another man. Swanny took his bat from the rack and stepped toward the plate.

Seized by a sudden impulse, Roy went across. It's now or never. If I don't do it now, I never will. It's now or never.

Casey saw him. He stepped forward.

"Hey . . . Casey . . . I wanna say . . . I wanna say I'm awful sorry about the other night in Cleveland."

The red-faced sportswriter grabbed his arm.

"Sorry, nuts! You got nothing to be sorry for. I'm the one should be sorry. Roy, I'm ashamed of what I said that night. It's not true, and you didn't need to show me up yesterday to prove it, either. Looka here, excuse me, will ya?"

"Excuse you? Nosir, excuse *me*."

They shook hands. The Kid was filled with a feeling of regret. The man's chest was big but his hand was flabby. He was soft and overweight and out of condition. And he was old, thirty or thirty-five maybe. Hitting a guy like that was hitting a child. He must have been insane. No decent person would have done such a thing. He was thoroughly disgusted with himself.

Casey went on talking. "All right. What say we forget the whole thing? But I'm glad you bopped me. I had it coming."

"Well, Casey, I'm mighty ashamed of myself for losing my temper, and I'm much obliged to you and all that, but I'd like for you to forgive me just the same."

"Sure, Roy. Of course. Sure thing. Now see here. Do me a favor, will ya?"

"You bet. What is it?"

"Just you go out there and act like you're Roy Tucker. Go out and play your game, your real game, I mean. Play the way you been playing all season. Heads-up ball. Go out and show these Cleveland mugs what you got. They think you're a soft touch, Roy!"

"You can't hardly blame 'em. You bet I will, Casey. And thanks, you've helped me lots. And I mean it, too."

He went to the bat rack, took his bat, picked up the heavy bat, and swinging them walked behind the cage. A cloud vanished over the horizon. There! That's over, over and done with. Now he could play ball.

Fat Stuff was in there throwing them up to the hitters. Imagine, after the shaking around he took yesterday, too. Some players never quit. Not Fat Stuff, for one. He's always in there. What a guy to have as an example on a team.

The Kid swung the bats in his hand, threw the leaded bat away, and stepped to the plate. The big leather ball bag was lying open on the ground between the box and second base, and Charlie Draper was feeding balls to Fat Stuff as fast as he threw them.

Well, that was over, anyhow. He stepped into the box feeling loose and easy. The first ball was right across, it was tagged. . . .

WHANG. It rose in the air, deep . . . deep . . . over the fence into Bedford Avenue.

Fat Stuff wasted the next one. Then he threw a curve which Roy fouled. He caught the next cleanly. Again the fielders backed up against the fence.

"Hey there, Tuck," called out Charlie Draper, "them balls cost MacManus money." There was a joyous note in his voice. He had noticed immediately the difference in the Kid's swing. That lad was loose once more. The whole team was loose. Now they'd move.

Roy sent one into deep center, stepped back from the box, and stood watching the fielders scuttle after it. He walked back to the dugout, seeing Dave on the bench in conversation with one of the Cleveland sportswriters. Dave was right all along about Casey. Dave was always right. Dave was his friend, the best in the business. Now they'd have to go out and win for Dave. They would, too. He'd play ball, heads-up baseball. The kind Casey wanted him to play.

Boy, bring on that man Thomas. Thomas, shucks! Bring on Gene Miller!

10

Dave sat in the dugout surveying his team, watching the men at bat, keeping an eye on the fielders chasing fungoes.

"Rog," he called down the bench. "Tell someone to relieve Fat Stuff. The old boy's tired."

"I'll tell you, George . . ." He continued talking to one of the Cleveland sportswriters he had known in other days, but all the while he was sweeping the field with his eyes, missing nothing that happened. Dave on some subjects was uncommunicative. When, however, it was a matter of young players he himself had trained and brought along, he was apt to be expansive. "I'll tell you one thing. He isn't overrated the way you folks think; fact is, he's underrated. Why, you fellas haven't seen him yet; maybe you won't, maybe he won't come out of it this year after that beaning. But I sure wish I could do some of the things he does. There! D'ja see that? D'ja see him come in there and take that sinker off his shoes?"

"Yeah." Grudgingly. "Oh, he's fast, all right, all right."

"He's fast and he's got a pair of hands. 'Nother thing, he's a hustler. Take it from me he's in there every second. After each inning he comes back here to the dugout with the same question; 'Did I make the right throw then, Dave?' 'Did I play that man right, Dave?' And I don't need to holler at him, either. He's always watching when a hitter comes up. Just between you and me that's one reason I had to let Scudder go last season. Now this boy isn't that way. I give it to him once and he has it for good. First game . . . no, wait a minute . . . first game he played in Cleveland it was, I moved him toward center for Hammy. When Lanahan comes up I shove him over to the foul line. Next game I don't even have to signal. That's the kind of ball he plays. . . . Why, Harry! Hullo, Harry, how are you? It's good to see you again."

An older man advanced into the dugout, hand extended. "Hullo there, Dave. Good to see you, too. How's everything?"

"Just fine, Harry, except we can't seem to hit these Cleveland pitchers. How's tricks with you out on the Coast?" The Cleveland reporter listened to the two old friends talking. You never knew when you would learn something which would be valuable.

"Congratulations, Dave! Your boys are putting up a grand good fight."

"Congratulations my eye! We haven't begun to play our game yet."

"Considering you got one of your best men beaned in the first game and your catcher's been out the whole Series, I think you're doing first rate. How's it feel, Dave, to be back in there again?"

"Well, it was tough at first. Every time I bent down to give the signal I could feel it all over my body. Bones would creak and muscles groan until I figured I'd been wired for sound. But the worst thing of all, Harry, were those high fouls. The first game I caught, everything was swell until the ninth. I'd had one pop but it was right over my head, didn't move out of the box. I

began to think catching had become easier
since I quit. Then came the ninth.

"First guy rolled out. Next man hits a high
foul and I had to run way over to our dugout to
get it. You can imagine how high it must have
been when I finally grabbed it. That left me
winded and tired out, and I stalled around
before going to work on the next batter. What's
he do? Darned if he doesn't hit another high one
that carries me over to their bench. I can't tell
you how or why, but I got that one, too. Afterward they almost had to carry me off the field. I
took a good hot salt bath last night for an hour,
but just the same I got a couple of bad charley
horses this morning. . . ."

The bell rang. The Cleveland sportswriter rose
and sauntered across the field to the Indian
bench. Cleveland went into the field and the
Dodger dugout was filled with sweaty men in
uniform, slapping their bats in the rack, going
to the water cooler, or watching the Indian fielders throw to bases. Elmer was warming up with
West alongside Rats Doyle and Kennedy. Dave
still sat on the bench nursing his charley horses,
saving himself as much as possible. He needed
all the energy he could command.

On third base Al Schacht began clowning

around, running for a ball, falling on his face, trying to catch one with his silk hat, and generally drawing laughter from the crowd. Then suddenly the clown disappeared and there was that tense moment before the start, each man in both dugouts thinking of one thing—the difference between $6,400 and $4,400. As the papers had announced that morning, this was the difference between the winner's and the loser's share. And nearly every player had the same thoughts at the same time: my misplay may make that difference.

They swarmed from the dugout. In just a minute their voices chattered across the field from every position.

"Atta boy, Elmer. . . ."

"Okay Elmer-boy, le's go. . . ."

"Here's the easy man, Elmer. . . ."

The big pitcher smoothed the dirt from the front of the rubber and burned in his first pitch. Lanahan, the batter, hit it, a fast grounder which Harry scooped up and shot across to Allen. So the Indians weren't going to take the ball either! They were out to win from the start, too.

In the field the Kid watched Dave adjust his mask and go to work with Elmer on McClusky.

They pitched carefully, and finally he popped to Ed Davis back of second. Old Gardiner came loping to the plate. Gardiner, the Kid remembered, except in the second game, had been taking all through the Series, wearing down the Dodger pitchers as much as he could. Elmer would recall this also and would try to sneak over a first strike. Elmer did exactly that. And the veteran, catching the ball squarely, drove a hot liner over third for a clean single.

Crossed him up! That's the reason he's such a grand ballplayer, that man.

Two down, Kenny Rock at the plate. May be a hit-and-run. The Kid pulled the dirt from his spikes, adjusted the sunglasses pushed back over the visor of his cap, and stood ready for anything. On a ball team every man expects every ball to be hit at him and the Kid was no exception to this rule. He tried to figure what to do and where to throw on any kind of a hit ball.

A run sure would be bad for us now, he thought. It sure would.

Rock hit a rasping grounder to the left of first base. Red was over, reached it, knocked it down, and threw to McCaffrey covering first. But the pitcher, always a slow starter, lost the race for the bag.

Shoot! Two on and two out. Now that's bad! Why, we practiced that a million times. I've seen the pitchers practicing that play by the hour. He recalled the time in Clearwater in spring practice which they had devoted to that simple play. He could see Dave batting grounders from the box, the pitcher wheeling, running to first for the ball. This error might mean an important run because Hammy was at the bat; Hammy, the powerhouse of the Cleveland team. Fat Stuff would have had that man. Fat Stuff was heavier than McCaffrey, but he never made slips of that kind. No use worrying. No use thinking over others' mistakes. Let's go to work on Hammy.

Elmer pitched to him with care. He smoothed out the dirt before the rubber, hitched up his pants, and looked round the bases.

A strike, high inside. That's a good sign, thought the Kid. Shows Elmer's ahead of the hitters today. A ball, wide. He wound up; another ball wide of the plate, in fact very wide, yet Dave was ready for it. Without even shifting his stance he shot it to first. Rock was caught by a foot sliding back to the bag and the side was out.

Say what you like, Dave Leonard was a great ballplayer. He sure pulled Elmer out of that hole. "He certainly picked Elmer up that time, didn't he, Red?" Yessir. No wonder they all liked to pitch to Dave. He was always in there trying to help out his pitchers, to keep them in a good frame of mind.

"Nice work, Dave."

"Nice throwing there, Dave."

"Snappy work, Dave."

"All right now, gang, le's us go."

But they couldn't seem to get going. Red Allen grounded to the shortstop, and the Kid stepped to the plate. He caught the first pitch on the nose and drove it back hard at the man in the box who stuck out his glove and grabbed the ball before he could even get away from the plate. Hang it all! A little higher and it would have been a clean single.

"Shoot," he said, bouncing his bat on the plate. "Aren't we ever going to get any breaks at all?"

"It's not how hard you hit 'em, it's where you hit 'em in this man's game, sonny," said McCormick, the catcher, as he turned away.

"Yeah? All right, baby, we'll get to you guys yet; see if we don't."

Then Swanny flied to center and the inning was over.

McCaffrey was pitching well, but Dave continued to pull him out of holes. In the third Lanahan led off with another single, his second of the game. Elmer threw a wild pitch at McClusky, the next batter, that Dave knocked down. On first Lanahan was dancing away, not daring to risk the throwing arm of the old catcher. That would have meant another base if West had been in there, thought the Kid. It gave him confidence to see the fear Dave commanded in the opposing team.

On the next pitch McClusky grounded to Ed Davis who was obliged to throw to first to get the runner, with no chance of catching Lanahan at second. Old Fox Gardiner came up. He hit a looping ball . . . the Kid raced in. . . .

Can't make it. Too late ! Over the crowd's roar he heard Red and Davis both yelling at him. "Home . . . home! Home, Roy!" He took the ball on the second hop, all poised for the throw. From his place in short right he decided to throw all the way. The ball went on a line exactly where the veteran catcher straddled the plate. Lanahan, seeing the ball was waiting, made no effort to slide but struck Dave with the full force of his right shoulder and knocked him spinning in the dirt. Dave fell, still clutching the ball, and the runner was out. Some players might have dropped it; not Dave Leonard. The next batter flied to Karl and again Elmer was out of a bad hole. The Kid felt better as he came trotting into the dugout.

"That was the right throw on him, wasn't it, Dave?"

Cleveland finally managed to put a run over in the fourth, a run which kept looking bigger and bigger as the game progressed. A two thousand dollar run, it was. The way Thomas was pitching, that run was as good as ten. The Dodger batters were swinging ahead of the ball, sending easy grounders to third or short balls which the pitcher nabbed in time to get them at first. Dave tried not to fret. Surely they'd get one run. One run wasn't asking much. Then in the Cleveland sixth, Hammy got a curve on the business end of his forty ounce club and smashed it to deep center. When Swanny at last relayed it to the infield the big first baseman was puffing on third.

Bruce Gordon swinging three bats in his hand came to the plate. He fouled one into the stands and the Kid watched Dave take a new ball from Stubblebeard and throw it over to Jerry Strong on third. Jerry rubbed it up well before tossing it to Elmer. Jerry was the team's official rubber-up. They always threw him new balls.

Two strikes. Then two and one. Gordon hit the next, an easy grounder to Harry. Before his eyes the Kid had the whole panorama: Hammy cautiously retreating to third, Gordon straining for first, Harry at short set for the ball and all ready to throw.

Then! It struck a pebble, took a bad hop, and bounced over Harry's head into center field. Hammy scored standing up and the count was two to nothing.

My gosh, don't we ever have any luck? Don't we ever get any luck at all? A run like that, a scratch hit on what should have been an easy out! Two to nothing. Now the pressure will be on Elmer. One run is bad, two runs to get with only three innings left is tough. And this isn't over yet. There's Gordon on first and Painter, a dangerous man, at bat.

Dave and Elmer conferred together. Then they separated. A hit-and-run, possibly.

Yes, it was a hit-and-run. A clean hit, too. No! Eddie had the ball, way back of second. How the heck did he manage to get over there? He was on one foot, off balance, all tied up in knots, but somehow he got the ball away with that split second quickness so vital in doubleplays. Harry had it just as Gordon slid into the bag in a vain attempt to upset him. The little shortstop deftly sidestepped the spikes of the runner and burned the ball into first. Up went the hand of the umpire on second. Up went the hand of the umpire behind first. And up went the roar from the throats of thousands of fans. It was the first time the Dodger crowd had really had a chance to yell since the game began and they made the most of it. This was the Dodgers again.

End of the seventh. Those two runs looked big on the scoreboard over the Kid's head in right. Two runs; we need three but we'll settle for two. Who's up? Bottom of the batting order. Ed Davis at the plate. Here's hoping the boys save me a rap. Gee, I hope they save me a rap. My last rap of the game, maybe. Perhaps the last of the Series, he thought. Then with every other man on the bench he leaped to his feet. Ed was slinging his bat away. The first base on balls Thomas has given. He's weakening.

Dave at bat. A man on first and no one out. He touched his cap, wiped his right hand carefully on his trousers. The entire Cleveland team, knowing how badly a run was needed, were looking for anything. So on the pitch, as Ed dashed for second base, Gardiner went over to cover the bag. Dave, an experienced batter, waited until from one corner of his eye he saw Gardiner break. Then he cracked a lazy bounder straight through the open position between first and second. It was a clean hit. Ed slid easily into third and Dave planted himself on first. Now the entire dugout was on the step, yelling. Two men on, no one out. Two runs to make up!

The Kid went over to the bat rack for his stick. Yep, I'll get my rap all right. And if that old bird Leonard can hit this pitcher, by ginger I can. Here's our chance. This is our inning, fellas.

11

W in your own game, Elmer."

   "All right, now, Elmer, you can do it.

"Just a single, that's all we need, Elmer, old-boy-old-kid."

The dugout like the stands was in delirium. Every man was on his feet roaring from the step. Two runs behind. A hit meant a run this time. The Cleveland catcher and pitcher stood with their heads together in the middle of the path. Two runs behind. A hit would mean a run and another hit would tie the score. It was a bad situation for a pitcher.

Come on there, Elmer. Win your own game. He gripped the bat, attempted a bunt to score the man on third, but missed the ball completely. Shucks! Strike one. It silenced the dugout temporarily. Now he'll have to hit. A ball! More chatter from the dugout. Then a mighty shout in the bleachers. Two balls. Yessir, Thomas was weakening. The pitcher smoothed the dirt back of the rubber, hitched nervously at his pants, and passed his arm over his forehead. The battery was working carefully on Elmer, trying to get him to hit into a doubleplay, and the Kid, watching from the dugout, realized the two forces contending, each attempting to outguess the other. For a second he forgot the thousands of spectators above, the thousands of extra dollars at stake, forgot winning even, in watching the play and interplay which made baseball the game it was.

Suddenly there was a yell from the Cleveland dugout. He saw Dave and a cloud of dust arrive together at second. The old man had actually stolen a base with the Indian catcher completely napping. Dave had swiped second! What do you think of that? The idea that a slow, forty-year-old manager with, as they supposed, two charley horses, would dare go down, seemed impossible. The Cleveland team had been crossed beautifully. Men on second and third now.

That's better still. In the excitement he had
failed to notice the pitch. A glance at the
scoreboard showed the count 3-1. It was a ball.

All through the Series Dave had refused to
allow his pitchers to hit the 3-1 throw. This, he
felt, was percentage baseball. The man who
wasn't going to take could hit, but he ordered his
pitchers to take. The Kid watched him flash the
signal for Elmer to hit. It was a set-up play if, as
seemed probable, the catcher called for a
straight ball. He did. Elmer cracked it with all
the force of his powerful body deep into right
field. Gordon went back for the catch but didn't
try for the throw-in. One man down, a runner on
third, and one run across. Now they only had
one run to get. One run worth two thousand dollars to every player on the team.

Big Red Allen strode to the plate. He hit the
first ball sharply to the right of the second
baseman. Old Gardiner was slow getting across,
reached it late, stooped to pick it up, threw, and
the runner was safe. And Dave was over with the
tieing run!

There's our break! There's the break we had
coming. "Ed Davis would have had that one in
his pocket. Sure he would, wouldn't he, Karl?"
Never mind, we needed that break; it came just

at the right moment. Boy, if I can only hit one now we're really set.

He watched one pitch and caught the next. But he failed to meet it squarely. It struck the end of his bat and the ball looped over Painter's head for a scratch single into left field. Red Allen streaked to second.

A base on balls! Swanny trotted to first while out in the bullpen the two Cleveland pitchers stopped watching and began to concentrate earnestly on their warm-up throws.

Three on and only one out! They weren't done yet. Now, Karl! C'mon there, Karl! The Kid stood on second, watching Karl come confidently to the plate.

A hit! Oh, that was a hit! A clean liner into deep center. That ball is traveling. McClusky couldn't get that one with a motorcycle.

The Kid, head down, rounded third and dug for home, while Karl planted himself defiantly on second base. As Roy trotted across the plate, he observed the hot, disappointed face of the Cleveland catcher. He was holding his mask in his hand, shaking his head. The Kid couldn't resist jabbing him.

"It's not how hard you hit 'em, Mac, it's where

you hit 'em, hey?" The catcher heard but paid
no attention whatever.

Behind the plate, over opposite in the rear of
the Dodger dugout, in the stands in deep center,
the fans were on their feet, giving the raspberry
to the visiting team. This was something like!
The Cleveland players, their confidence gone,
their noisy chatter now subdued, stood watching as a relief pitcher hurried over from the
bullpen.

Harry Street hit the first pitch between short
and second, a sizzling grounder no one could
reach. Why, everyone was hitting at last. Then
Jerry Strong got a single and Ed Davis came to
bat for the second time that inning. When it was
over they had scored seven runs, eventually
knocking the Indian relief man from the box and
coming into the ninth with a safe lead. Elmer
allowed another run, but working carefully he
and Dave always had the situation under control. There were two out and a man on second
when Hammy came to the plate in the ninth.

The most dangerous man on the field. But
even a homer will only mean two runs, thought
Roy. Hammy hit hard. From the sound Roy
knew it was headed his way. He went back,
back, back as far as he could. The sun was in

his eyes, he could see nothing. He reached up his glove. . . . There it was! The game was over.

Instead of stopping, he wheeled and kept on running past the shrieking bleachers all the way to the clubhouse, his hand still uplifted, the ball clutched in his glove, a grin a mile wide on his face; while the fans were running to form lines at the box offices to buy tickets for the seventh game.

Meanwhile the team stormed into the dressing room. Clack-clack, clackety-clack. The ball was still stuck in the webbing of his glove.

"Boy, they'll have to take a hammer to get that one out." Someone was slapping him on the back. Someone else called across the room. Once again it resounded to shouts and laughter. The photographers were climbing on chairs and tables, on the tops of lockers, their flashlights popping. The Dodgers were still in the fight.

"Yippee . . . yippee!"

"Yippee! Who said we couldn't hit their pitchers?"

"Hey there, Chisel, you old slowfoot, gimme a Coke."

"Naw. We ain't started yet."

"Yippee. Yowser!"

"Nice going there, Elmer."

"That's chucking, Elmer."

The big pitcher seated on a table was sucking a Coke through a straw. Reporters surrounded him.

"What were you throwing out there today, Elmer?"

"Same stuff I been throwing for years. Mostly fast balls. I threw a few high neck-in pitches, and they got hungry."

"You sure poured it in those last few innings," said Dave. "Almost too fast for these old eyes."

"Yessir, Elmer, you pitched a grand game out there. They were stretching most of the time."

"Aw . . . when you got a catcher like Dave Leonard a man can't help coming through. He's with you all the time."

"That's right." This emphatic remark came from Charlie Draper who entered dragging the big leather ball bag. "Dave, you caught a darn fine game, I'll tell the world. A couple of those low pitches there in the sixth or seventh, if they'd got away we'd sure been out of luck."

"He pulled me through. Don't I know it," said Elmer.

"Who'll you pitch tomorrow, Dave?" As usual, Casey was on the job.

"Dunno. The man who's the whitest, I guess. The man who's most scared."

Old Chiselbeak circulated through the room, his face smiling and happy, catching wet garments thrown to him as the players got ready for the showers. More people came in. Across the big room the team shouted remarks.

"Congratulations, Roy."

"Nice work yourself, Eddie. How you ever got to that one in the sixth I dunno. It looked like a hit from my place."

"Shoot! We'll beat those birds tomorrow. Yes, sir, Miller and all of 'em."

"We sure will."

"Yippee . . . yippee. . . ."

"Great work, fellas."

"Thanks lots, Pete. Thanks, Casey."

Back in his dressing room off the main quarters, Dave with a cigarette in his mouth began to undress. He was tired. No fooling, he was tired. The strain of playing and running the team and holding the pitchers together was telling. He felt he couldn't face up to the next day. His thighs and legs ached. His muscles were sore all over. Slowly he threw off his shoes and started to pull down his pants when he found himself surrounded by a circle of reporters. The Dodgers had won. True, but old man Leonard was the story. Old man Leonard who pulled a shaky pitcher through to triumph, who caught a grand game of ball, who started the rally that won, and who at forty actually stole second under the eyes of the best catcher in the American League.

Dave was the angle. They'd have to concentrate on Dave. More men entered and he glanced up at the growing circle, the reporters with pads out, some with folded paper, all with pencils at the ready. There were Casey and one or two more columnists, there were Rex King of the *Times*, bespectacled and kindly, quick-witted Sandy Martin of the *Post*, big Jerry Regan of the *Tribune*, Dennison of the *News*, as well as lots of Cleveland writers he had never seen before. A mob of them! It was a formidable assembly.

He paused, sitting there on his four-legged stool, his trousers half-on, half-off.

"Don't tell me you bums want me to give you a story tonight. Get out of here, the whole lot of you. Go into the big room there and talk to the boys. They're the ones that did the work."

12

Dave was tieing his necktie before a cracked mirror in his dressing room. This cracked mirror dated from the time twenty years before, when as a cub he had broken in with the White Sox. Everywhere he went he carried the cracked glass and hung it on the wall of his quarters.

"Charlie . . ."

Charlie Draper on a stool, thick in conversation with Cassidy, looked up. He saw Dave motioning with his head, rose and went over to the manager. Finishing his tie, the old catcher said in an undertone:

"Charlie, I want you should see how many players are going to the banquet tonight."

"Yeah, Dave. I stuck that notice on the board."

"No, no. That won't do any good. I want you should round them up, personal-like. Make 'em feel they oughta show up. Point is, they don't want to go. But I'd rather they did. You can't send players to bed at ten o'clock, that'll only increase the pressure on 'em."

"But looka here, Dave; I spoke to one or two of the boys. They somehow just don't want to go."

" 'Course they don't. That's your job. You must persuade 'em. Otherwise, Charlie, they'll spend their time thinking about tomorrow. They come to dinner and pick up a menu with their faces all over the cover. Then they go into the lobby to be pestered by autograph nuts, or take in a movie and tire their eyes out, or sit all evening in their room reading newspapers and tightening up over this-here game. I want them at that banquet where their minds won't be on the game. For a while, anyhow."

So Charlie with a pad and pencil went dutifully around the room. He didn't have a great deal of luck.

"What banquet?" asked Rats Doyle, with

scorn in his voice. He had played in other Series and been to other banquets.

"Nuts," said Harry Street, struggling into his coat. "I got something better to do than go to banquets."

"How 'bout you, Razzle?"

"Naw. I have a date tonight."

From player to player, always the same response. They were busy, they were bored, they were not having any banquets. The Kid began to feel sorry for the people running the banquet, and as Charlie, pad and pencil in hand, went around the room, he changed his mind. He'd go. Fat Stuff was going also. Apparently he and Fat Stuff would represent the team that evening.

What kind of a banquet was it? At the bulletin board near the door he paused as he went out and read a letter pinned there.

"The Chamber of Commerce in conjunction with Martin Motors, Inc. requests the pleasure of the company of the members of the Brooklyn National League Baseball Club at a dinner to be held in their honor at the Hotel Morton on the evening of Tuesday, October 6th." Now that was mighty nice of those folks. Roy felt glad he had accepted. You try to be kind, to arrange a feed and show appreciation of the team's pull-up, and then nobody takes the trouble to attend. That's ballplayers for you!

Outside and down the ramp. The game had been over almost an hour but a few stragglers hung round the wire netting, watching the players emerge. Red Allen was standing at one side talking to a group of ladies. His wife was there and Fat Stuff's wife and several other ladies including a blonde in furs. That might be Razzle's girl.

They looked at him curiously as he went out the exit and past them, immediately to be assailed by a bunch of boys, pads, notebooks, scorecards extended. For ten minutes he stood there signing his name, the group seeming never to diminish. Finally he worked his way through. No, not quite.

"And mine . . ."

"And mine, please . . ."

"Aw, please, Mr. Tucker . . . "

"Mr. Tucker, just one more, please . . . "

He knew some of them were repeaters. They were doubling up on him; one autograph for themselves and one for trading purposes. However, having started, he had to continue. Gradually he worked his way toward the gate, still pursued, still signing.

"Taxi . . ."

"Taxi, mister?"

"Hotel Nevada." He sank back and slammed the door, almost taking off the fingers of several autograph hounds. The car moved away and he realized how tired he was. Tired, even though they'd won. You were more tired when you lost, to be sure, yet he was tired. The nervous tension was what took it out of you; the mental straining, the hoping, the anxiety, the effort of body and will to pull a game out when the score and the chances were all against you. For just a moment he contemplated an early supper and going to bed. Then he knew he wouldn't rest. He'd lie in bed going over that game the next day. Besides he had promised and he'd have to show up. It would be a dirty trick to walk out if only a couple of them were attending. At the hotel he paid the taxi, went through the crowded lobby, faces turning as he passed, bought some newspapers and took the elevator to his room.

On one bed was Harry's laundry, carefully laid out with a slip, waiting to be counted and checked by its owner. But no Harry. Then the telephone rang.

"Hullo."

"That you, Harry?"

"Nope, this isn't Harry, it's Roy. Harry isn't here yet."

"Oh." The speaker rang off.

Now that's funny. Funny too that Harry wasn't there. By rights he should be in the room going over his laundry and grumbling because a pair of pajamas or his green shirt hadn't been returned. The Kid looked at his watch. Three-thirty. Stopped. Must have forgotten to wind it. He took up the telephone.

"Give me the right time, please."

"The correct time is . . . five forty-two."

Quarter to six! And no Harry. That's strange. Where could he be? The Kid took off his coat, lay down on the bed, and opening a newspaper glanced at the pictures. A snap of the field and Kenny Rock sliding into first in a column of dust; Eddie back of second, poised for the throw to Harry, with Gordon straining for the bag. Then his own figure racing for the dugout, left arm extended, the ball shown with a white arrow. Wonderful pictures they took nowadays. Wonderful, yessir.

The telephone jingled again. "A telegram for you, Mr. Tucker. Shall we send it up?"

Now what? Grandma? No, she had refused to come down. She wasn't, she said, traveling to Brooklyn to see Roy hit on the head with a baseball. It was quite bad enough to hear about it over the radio. Well, maybe she'd changed her mind. He dug out a quarter and had it ready when the boy knocked.

"Thanks. And, Mr. Tucker, would you mind giving me your signature here . . . on this white paper here?"

Roy signed for the telegrams, signed the white paper also, and took the envelopes, for there were two. He opened one.

"IN EVENT VICTORY TOMORROW WOULD YOU BE INTERESTED APPEARING TED FALLON HOUR OVER NBC NETWORK THURSDAY NIGHT NINE STOP FEE SEVEN HUNDRED FIFTY STOP IF AGREEABLE WILL HAVE REPRESENTATIVE CALL YOUR HOTEL PLEASE CONFIRM JAMES C PARSONS ROCKEFELLER CENTER."

Whew. He tore open the other envelope. It was from Chicago.

"GENERAL STORES OFFERS YOU TWO THOUSAND FOR YOUR ENDORSEMENT ITS GROCERY PRODUCTS IN EVENT TEAM VICTORY AND YOU BAT OVER THREE TWENTY FIVE PETER J KINGDOM VICE PRESIDENT."

Whew again! He sat down quickly on the bed. Then he rose and sat down on a chair. Then he went over to the window, saw nothing, came back and sat down on the bed again. You couldn't endorse cigarettes when you never smoked, but he supposed he ate General Stores' groceries. He certainly did at home; he remembered buying them in the village for Grandma.

Let's see now; seven fifty, that makes fifty-two sixty, that makes, no, wait a minute, that makes . . . He went to the desk and wrote down:

Series	$6,400
Ted Fallon	750
General Stores . .	2,000
	$7,150

No. That wasn't right. Why, he couldn't even add straight. $9,150, not $7,150. Nine thousand one hundred and fifty bucks on one ball game. On one inning, maybe, on a catch in the field, or a scratch single at the plate. And perhaps the other way round; on one of their catches in the field or one of their scratch singles. All that dough, more than he had made from his two seasons in the majors, on one game alone. On one inning, one lucky stab in the field.

He grabbed a newspaper and turned to the sports pages where the batting averages of both teams were listed. His eye skimmed the column. Case . . . Swanson . . . Street . . . Allen . . . Tucker . . . there it was, Tucker . . . now, he was .272 the day before . . . and .285 tonight.

.285. Well, if he got a couple of hits tomorrow, say two out of two, and that wasn't impossible, that would make . . . no, wait a minute. Miller would be pitching tomorrow. How would he do against Miller? Would he tighten up and get scared or be loose and easy in the box against him?

The telephone rang. It had, he realized, been ringing some time.

"Hullo."

"Harry Street? Street there?"

"Nope. He isn't. He ought to be, though, any minute." The speaker rang off. A vaguely familiar voice, but Roy was far too excited to pay much attention. Over nine thousand dollars! Enough to put electricity on the farm, to oil the road up from the state highway, to get Grandma the new electric stove and a Frigidaire, too. All on a single game. On one single inning, maybe.

Well, he couldn't go on this way. It would tighten him up and he'd be so jittery he'd be useless the next afternoon. So he lay down on the bed, arranged the pillow, and tried to read the newspapers. Yesterday's game. It seemed a thousand years ago. The account was stale, dull reading. But there were pictures—of Dave in the dressing room, his pants half down and a cigarette in his mouth; of Fat Stuff rolling on the ground in pain. Then there was the mix-up at the plate. That must be Karl and No. 6, that was Swanny. Doesn't look like him, though. And there was his own back with the big 34, half rising from the circle, his bat in one hand. He turned to Casey's column and started reading.

"There's no quit in the Dodgers. This bunch of gamesters outfought . . . " The telephone jingled once more.

"Hullo. Raz Nugent there?"

"Nugent? Nope, he's in 1235."

"Oh! Thought he was in there." The speaker rang off. That was funny. The same familiar voice. He went back to Casey and the newspaper.

"Yesterday the vaunted Indians looked like fugitives from a Class AA League, while the Dodgers were the Dodgers of old. That ancient mariner, Dave Leonard, who's hardly as fast on his feet as Paul Whiteman and about twice as old, stole second under the eyes of McCormick and the Cleveland fielders. The last time Dave stole a base was when Pershing took Chateau-Thierry. Roy Tucker came to life out in right and speared the ball in his old-time fashion, and the whole team played heads-up baseball. But it was Ed Davis who really came through for the Flatbush gangsters. He covered more ground than a tarpaulin and handled a gaudy total of ten chances in the field, and his run in the 7th set the Brooks back in the game and the fight for the Series. He also started two doubleplays with the bases as loaded as a shoplifter's pocket. All in all, if anyone tries to tell you this isn't a game team, call a cop."

"Come in, come in . . ." Suddenly Roy came out of his dream to realize that someone was knocking at the door.

The door opened and Fat Stuff stood there with Jerry Strong. It was not the queer, barrel-chested figure in the monkey suit with the long arms hanging from his flannel shirt, but a tanned gentleman in evening clothes. Jerry, too, was all dressed up.

"Hey, there, Kid. Aren't you going to the banquet tonight?"

"Sure, I am."

"Well, you better climb into your soup and fish, then. They're calling for us in about twenty minutes."

"Gosh!" He jumped up, hurriedly ransacking his drawers for a shirt, a collar, and a black tie. "Here, Fat Stuff, be a good guy, will ya? Put those studs in for me."

The telephone rang again. "I'll answer," said Jerry, who was the only unoccupied person in the room. "Hullo. Who? Nugent? Why, no, this isn't Nugent's room. . . ."

"1235," the Kid shouted from the bathroom. "Tell him Nugent hasn't been here since the game."

"He's in 1235. This is Tucker and Street here. Well, I'll be darned. He rings off in my ear." Jerry replaced the telephone. "That's funny. Seems as if I knew that voice."

Down in the lobby they found Dave dressed and waiting for them with Elmer McCaffrey near the desk. A bellboy came through the crowd. "Mr. Dave Leonard. Calling Mr. Leonard. . . ."

"Here you are, right here, boy."

"Mr. Leonard? Long distance call for you, sir.

If you like you can take it here on the desk."
Dave turned and removed a telephone by his
elbow. Standing beside him the Kid heard his
first words.

"Hullo . . . yep . . . all right, put her on here
. . . hullo . . . hullo, Helen . . . yes, we did all
right, didn't we . . . sure . . . we sure did . . .
uhuh. . . . I don't know why not . . . yes . . .
nothing definite yet. . . . I say I haven't anything to tell you so far. . . ."

Roy didn't want to hear any more. He turned
away. Dave was talking to his wife about next
season. Evidently MacManus hadn't signed him
up. It all depended on that game. He forgot his
endorsements and the Ted Fallon hour and the
rest of it. They'd have to go out and powder that
ball for Dave. By gosh, they'd win on that field
for Dave Leonard; they'd make him manager
next year.

13

MacManus had the Kid's arm in a vise-like grip. Boy, was that man strong!

"And this is Roy Tucker, my right fielder, Mr. Jameson. I wouldn't trade him for any right fielder in either league today." He dropped the Kid's arm, and leaning over, his face close to the other man's, tapped his chest. "No, sir. Not for Masters or Benny Rogers or Dan Pike, even. You can have 'em. The whole lot. I'll take this lad." He glared at the stout gentleman, as if anxious to be contradicted. The stout man merely held out his hand.

"Glad to meet you, Mr. Tucker. It's good of you to come here tonight, and we're happy to have you with us." Roy felt more ashamed than ever that the rest of the team had walked out on the party. Moreover he was dazzled into silence by MacManus and his eloquence. But chiefly by MacManus.

Jack was dressed for the occasion. The ball-players—Dave, Jerry, Fat Stuff, McCaffrey, and he himself—all wore tuxedos and black ties. So did the majority of the diners who were to sit at the long table raised above the rest of the huge ballroom. But that wasn't good enough for Jack MacManus. He wore a dress suit. His big chest filled out the coat, his white tie was immaculate, and a red carnation in his buttonhole added a finishing touch that made the others, now moving to their seats, seem almost shabby.

"For my money," whispered Elmer in his ear as they took their places near the toastmaster at the head table, "for my money he's as good as Clark Gable." To which the Kid earnestly agreed. No doubt about it.

The big hall was festooned with flags, pennants, bunting, and banners bearing the inscription: BROOKLYN BASEBALL CLUB. NATIONAL LEAGUE CHAMPIONS. Others bore the sign: WE WELCOME THE WORLD'S CHAMPS. It was indeed a festive occasion. The gentlemen of the Chamber of Commerce had done things in good style, with huge bunches of roses on the tables, a menu tied in colored string, pictures of the team on one cover, and souvenirs in the shape of baseballs at their plates. The Kid opened his ball and there in a satin cover was a wrist watch, presented by Lowells, Inc., Jewelers, of Atlantic Avenue. The name of each player, the date, and the event were engraved on the back. Maybe Grandma wouldn't open her eyes when she saw that watch!

"Baby! That'll sure come in handy," remarked Elmer. "I dropped mine in the shower the other day and bust it completely."

"Me, too. Mine's been stopping every little while lately. It's all worn out." The Kid took the gold watch from the satin cover inside the baseball, looked at it carefully, and slipped it on his wrist.

"Hey, Roy . . . " Fat Stuff leaned toward him, his red face beaming. "Won't Rats Doyle be burned up he didn't come when he spots these watches?"

"Will he! . . . "

"Yeah, and Razzle, too. Won't Raz be sore he kept that date with his blonde."

"I'll say. That's some watch."

They laid their presents aside and addressed themselves to the serious business of eating. The Kid slowly lost some of his uneasiness, though he still felt unpleasant and uncomfortable on that platform before the crowd, with those hundreds of eyes below staring at him. He dipped into his soup. "Hey there, Fat Stuff, you know everything. What's this soup?"

"Turtle soup."

"Turtle soup?"

"Yeah. Didn't you ever eat turtle soup in Florida at the training camp?"

"Nope. It's good, isn't it? Well, if you know so much, what's that—there on the menu?" He spelled out the words. "B-o-m-b-e D-o-d-g-e-r. There! What's that mean?"

"Dunno. Prob'ly some kind of ice cream, see, sort of fancy, all fixed up and named for the Dodgers. That's the way they always do at these banquets." Fat Stuff who had been in other Series knew the banquet technique.

The Kid was impressed. It was one thing to know the weakness of every hitter in the league or to get over to the bag before the runner on a hit to the first baseman. But to know the terms and technology of banqueting showed experience indeed.

"Like that peach thing we had in Dave's room in Cleveland the other night?"

"Better, better," said Fat Stuff, handing his watch to his wife who inspected it with a proprietary air and tried it on before returning it.

Better than the peach thing! Roy couldn't believe that. But he had to admit the dinner was good. Yes, the dinner was all right. Chicken and wild rice and string beans and salad and then the dessert. The dessert was ice cream in the shape of a bat and a ball. It was green pistachio, red strawberry, and white vanilla with loads of whipped cream all over it.

At the end of the table he caught a glimpse of MacManus talking to the white-haired gentleman next to him. Jack was talking with his whole body, his arms, his hands, tapping the man's chest and emphasizing his points. His ice cream was melting and the bat already had a wilted look. Why, that guy would rather talk than eat ice cream. Once served, the Kid attacked his immediately. It was as good as it looked.

Then someone was knocking on the table. The white-haired gentleman arose, several slips of paper in his hand. There was a scraping of chairs on the floor below, cigars and cigarettes were passed round and lighted. Boy, did Razzle miss it! Imagine, a free cigar for Raz. The Kid took one and put it beside his place to save for the big pitcher. But Fat Stuff was too quick. He reached over and grabbed the cigar, stuffing it into his pocket.

"Hey, Kid, you don't smoke. I'll just use that to celebrate tomorrow."

By this time the white-haired man was going on all six cylinders. "Fine representatives of this great city . . . magnificent sportsmen . . . brought new renown to our town. . . ." His remarks were spattered with interruptions of applause.

"Now I shall call on our fellow townsman, a gentleman you all know, Mr. Harry J. Martin of Martin Motors, Incorporated, who has an announcement to make."

Mr. Martin was a short, nervous and fussy little person. He tapped his cigar continually on a plate before him as he rose to slight clapping. There was more scraping of chairs on the floor below and people began looking round toward the rear of the room. Then, for the first time, Roy noticed two large draped mounds in the

back of the hall. Evidently something was about
to happen.

"On behalf of the Ford Motor Company which
I have the honor to represent in this district, and
also on behalf of Martin Motors, I want to say we
here in Brooklyn are proud to have with us
tonight these splendid representatives of the
best in baseball." Cheers from all over the room.
"We have, what is more, complete confidence
that they'll bring us the championship tomorrow
. . . that they will go out there . . ." His words
were lost in the noise. "And win!" He emphasized this statement. *"And win!"* Roy wished he
was as certain of it as Mr. Martin.

The nervous little man passed his finger inside
his collar, tapped his cigar on the plate before
him, and looked at a small paper in his hand. "I
regret . . . that is, Mr. Jameson of the Chamber
of Commerce and I regret that this dinner had to
be arranged on such short notice that it was
impossible for all the players to be with us.
However, as you see, we have a goodly number. . . ." Cheers, during which he consulted
the paper again. "We have, however, a goodly
number present, and I want you to meet them.
Beside me here, of course, you all recognize our
old friend. . . ." He turned toward MacManus.

Applause burst spontaneously through the hall. Jack MacManus was a Brooklyn favorite, no stranger to anyone in the room. He rose, erect, his sandy hair brushed off his face, and stood calmly smiling to the applauding crowd. Gosh, he was better than Clark Gable, at that! For a minute the owner of the Dodgers stood there, his napkin in one hand, his cigar in the other, pleasantly acknowledging the cheers of the crowd in an easy manner, completely successful, completely certain of himself. Then bowing to each side, he sat down before the applause had died away.

"The next man . . . hardly needs any introduction either. We've seen him here in Brooklyn when things were going well, when things were not going well, and when things were going very badly indeed. We've all watched him, watched him out there trying hard as a player, as a coach, and then as a great leader and inspiration for the gang of boys who hold the National League pennant today. Last of all, we see him again with pride as an actor in the drama which goes to its conclusion tomorrow, a happy conclusion for us all, I'm sure you'll agree, so I don't need . . . I . . . you all know . . ."

He couldn't continue. The noise was too

much. It echoed and re-echoed across the room;
it drowned out his voice, every man and woman
clapping. Then the Kid noticed someone rising,
hands moving, and then another and another.
Soon the entire room was on its feet, yelling. For
ages they stood, paying tribute to the manager of
the Dodgers.

14

He stood there, serious, grave, his brown eyes shining in his tanned face as he glanced from one side of the big room to the other. Still they stood clapping, showing their affection. Finally they stopped and sat down. He bowed quickly and resumed his seat.

Say, that was something! That was a tribute to a grand guy. That would show MacManus what the fans in Brooklyn thought of Dave Leonard. That was great, that was wonderful, that was grand. It made the Kid happy and warm all over. The crowd below hadn't clapped any harder than the five members of the team on the platform.

The speaker continued. "Back in 1935 I recall

seeing a great game in the Series between Detroit and St. Louis. It was a ten inning game and finally ended in a victory for the Tigers, two to one. The battery for that game was . . . Foster and Leonard." Applause again. He had no need to continue.

Fat Stuff, red-faced and uneasy, rose quickly and as quickly sat down. He was accustomed to banquets but not to public appearances at banquets.

"One of the members of this great team you don't hear much about . . . don't see his name in the papers making spectacular plays . . . but he's always in there. . . ." Good! He's gonna give Jerry Strong some credit. About time, too. Yes, sir, Jerry sure has it coming to him. Now there's one man we can depend on. Jerry rose and like Fat Stuff quickly subsided. Now the speaker got along to the Kid. He hardly heard what was being said.

". . . and a great favorite of our fellow-citizens in the bleachers out there in right . . . just heard Jack MacManus say this evening . . . and not for Benny Rogers or Danny Pike of the White Sox either. . . ."

The chair scraped behind him and he stood, staring into an ocean of curious faces. Then he hastily sat down. That was one part of the evening that was no fun at all.

The nervous little man continued. "Now, ladies and gentlemen, we have a surprise for you all this evening. As I said, we greatly regret that the whole team was unable to be with us, but I'm sure you'll agree we have a fine representation from the great-hearted bunch which has brought so much fame and honor to our municipality this season. So, on behalf of Martin Motors, it gives me much pleasure . . ." He fumbled and found his paper on which he had evidently written this part of his discourse. "It gives me much pleasure on behalf of Martin Motors and the fans of the city of Brooklyn, to present you, Dave Leonard, with our sincere best wishes . . . okay there, Spike. . . ." This last remark was to someone in the rear. The room suddenly darkened and a spotlight framed the cloth-covered bulk at the end of the hall, while two men ran around, yanking and pulling at strings. All at once the cloth fell away. There was a new, shiny automobile!

Cheers. More cheers. Again Dave rose, bowing, smiling his appreciation. Gosh! What do you think of that? "Hey, Fat Stuff, what is it? A Lincoln? Sure, it's a Lincoln, isn't it, Jerry?"

The little man continued: "We also have a tribute for the other members of the team with us tonight, ladies and gentlemen. Although we regret that it was impossible to bring five cars into the space at our disposal, the sample provided will give you an idea of the kind of transportation that . . . that the Messrs . . ." he fumbled with his paper . . . "that the Messrs Foster, Strong, Tucker, and McCaffrey will be riding in next season. Okay, Spike."

Once more the lights went off, the spot framed the other bulk in the rear of the room, and after some pulling the cloth fell away to disclose a baby blue sports roadster, shiny and resplendent in the glare. Then lights once more, while the four players rose, bowing awkwardly amid cheers and applause. The car, its hood back, stood neat and trim in the rear of the room. A Ford V8! The Kid recalled his first trip to the training camp, how from the train he had seen Raz Nugent riding in opulence along the Florida roads in an open car. And how he had longed and hoped for a blue roadster like that himself some day. Now he had it.

They whispered among themselves. "Oh boy, will Raz be burned up. Imagine missing a new car."

"And wait 'til Rats Doyle sees this."

"And Case."

"Yeah, and Harry Street." At the mention of Harry's name the Kid felt a twinge of regret. Hang it, he should have found Harry and dragged him along. If Harry had only shown up in the room at his usual time he could have come. It was a darn shame to miss out on a new car like this. Well, that's luck. Lucky for him he hadn't quit and gone to bed right after dinner as he felt like doing on leaving the ballpark that afternoon.

The little man sat down, beaming, and the white-haired toastmaster was on his feet. "A few more words . . . I know you'll all want to hear what he has to say . . . no need of any introduction . . . the man who has brought baseball back to Brooklyn after twenty years. . . ." Loud applause and cheers all over the room as MacManus arose. Strong, virile, handsome in his tails, the carnation on his chest, he surveyed the ballroom with an assurance that was almost impudence.

Just as he began speaking, Roy noticed three

painters near the door. At any rate they looked like painters or workmen of some kind. They wore white, paint-spotted overalls and white caps down over their ears, and they carried brushes and pots of paint in their hands. Then they brought in two long ladders. Oblivious to the festive hour, to the assembly in gala attire, to the high table with its famous men, even to the words of Jack MacManus, they went to work. Apparently the room was to be changed over for some other purposes and they had orders to start immediately.

Never at a loss for one word or a hundred, MacManus jumped into his talk with an easy, informal style. Unlike the other speakers, he needed no notes or written material or slips of paper to remind him of what he wished to say. With cool confidence, certain of the eager attention of his listeners, he went on in witty manner to describe the trials and difficulties of bringing top class baseball to a town that for years had been steeped in tailenders. Words flowed from his lips. Wisecracks sprinkled his sentences. The crowd ate it up.

But the trio of painters had no time or attention for his eloquence. They had a job to do. Dragging their ladders and pails across the floor, they managed to hit the leg of a table, knocking down the glassware with a clatter. Some hard looks were thrown their way and Jack, pausing for a second, surveyed their movements with an eye calculated to terrify them. Intent on their job, they never noticed him; so he was forced not to notice them. By much shoving and hauling they finally got their pails and ladders back of the speakers' table and behind the toastmaster. The white-haired man jumped up, and Roy could hear him arguing with them in a whisper.

"Gentlemen . . . gentlemen . . . wait a minute . . . please. . . ."

But they paid no heed except to shove a paper, which Roy guessed contained their orders, under his nose. "We can start here," said the big one in a tone everyone could hear.

The toastmaster, ruffled and irate, jumped down from the platform. "Waiter, send for the manager. Get the manager here at once." The waiter scuttled off, as with a loud WHANG the ladders were planted against the wall right over Jack's head.

One man mounted the unsteady, swaying thing. Then he hastily climbed down, having forgotten something. That drew titters throughout the room, and Jack's eloquence began to have less effect. The big man of the trio climbed up again, this time with a hammer in his hand, while most of the diners, fascinated, kept their eyes on his movements. He turned at the top and after a minute whistled through his teeth, making signs frantically to the others below. The titters became subdued laughter.

MacManus turned round, pausing, and looked them over with that cool insolence which was his. Unfortunately insolence was lost on these men who refused to notice him. Jack, unnoticed, was not entirely happy. Meanwhile the white-haired toastmaster, now red-faced and angry, was scuttling about the room. The speaker tried to continue.

"I was saying, I set my heart on a pennant for Brooklyn this year. So what? So did half a dozen other club owners, most of whom had bigger pocketbooks than I had." Gradually his charm, his refusal to get annoyed, his smooth delivery, and his wisecracks drew the crowd back. His magnetism was winning the day. He went on, his head thrust forward, talking with his arms, his big chest, his fists, his whole body.

"Yeowk . . . " There was a frightful screech from above as the big painter yanked one of the festooned banners from the wall with the claw of his hammer. "Yeowk . . . yeowk. . . ." It continued until the bunting hung at a tipsy angle, and the shield read like this:

THE WORLDS CHAMPIONS.
LEAGUE CHAMPIONS, WE WELCOME
BROOKLYN BASEBALL CLUB NATIONAL

MacManus was now obliged to pause. "If you boys there can only be patient until we beat the Indians tomorrow . . . " This sally drew applause. The crowd was all for him. Not the painters, however, who took no notice whatever of his pleas. He might have been addressing the wall. Another ladder was set up. The little painter, violently chewing gum, climbed up and yanked at the other end of the festooned bunting.

"Yeowk . . . Yeowk . . . Yeowk . . ."

CRASH. With a fearful noise, half the decorations fell in a heap behind the table, almost decapitating MacManus and the toastmaster. Now the suave speaker was annoyed. At first he had been mildly amused; now he was furious.

"Hey, there! Whatsa matter with you men?" The suaveness was gone, he was ruffled. The toastmaster, the president of Martin Motors, and the head waiter meanwhile were running from door to door in search of the manager, the assistant manager, the night clerk, or anyone in authority who could and would call off the renovating of the room until the banquet was finished. To the painters orders were orders and MacManus was just another man in a soup and fish. They wanted to be done with their work and get home to bed.

They stood looking down at their handiwork, not in the least apologetic, so MacManus was forced to continue. It became a kind of game between the speaker and the three workmen, and the speaker began to lose some of his poise and show some of his Irish by the flushing of his broad face. A shade of red crept above the nose, into his forehead. He was angry. Jack MacManus angry was a dangerous customer. Unfortunately the workmen didn't realize this fact.

"So, 's I say, I was saying . . . " He turned and glared at the painters, a glare which was lost because they were now on the floor with their heads together, mixing some paint in a pot. "So 's I say, I was trying to say, that is, we had the problem of getting a completely new outfield and some good pitchers. My infield I was satisfied with, so long as I had old Spencer at short, because Red Allen and Ed and Jerry here were just about as quick getting the ball away as any infield in the league. One day that summer, I was up at Waterbury, Connecticut . . . "

Oh, my gosh! Was he gonna tell that story again? Why, he'd told that story eight hundred times. The Kid groaned to himself.

"I was up in Waterbury there looking over a cub shortstop, boy by the name of Simpson; seemed as if he'd do for a utility fielder. The Cuban Giants were playing an exhibition game that afternoon, and there was a young pitcher in the box for Waterbury who held 'em to one hit. Right away I saw his possibilities. So I went to the manager, man by the name of Tommy Andrews. 'Tom,' I said, 'I'll give you exactly . . . ' "

Now MacManus was vaguely aware that this story, which was usually listened to with respectful attention, was not getting the complete interest of his audience. He was not sure why, but he could observe fascinated looks following the antics and actions of the men at his rear. Up one ladder went the big painter with a pot of paint on one arm and a brush in the other hand. The second painter climbed the second ladder. The remaining man held this ladder, but the big man had no one to steady his, and as a consequence it swayed dangerously as he climbed. Up, up he went, the ladder swaying, while from below:

"Ten thousand smackers . . . yes, sir, ten thousand dollars in the bank tomorrow morning at nine o'clock. And Tommy said, 'Well, Jack, the kid's gotta lot of possibilities; but ten thousand dollars is a *lotta dough.*' "

Now the ladder was swaying back and forth. Only a painter accustomed to climbing could have kept his balance. Actually he was having a time keeping his balance.

"LOOK OUT THERE, BUDDY. . . ." The big man on the top rungs was almost slipping and the paint pot on his arm was perilously near to upsetting. He was slipping. He was slipping! He reached out, caught the bunting and saved himself from a fall, but dropped the paint. It described an arc in the air, and while the gaze of five hundred benumbed diners followed it, descended on the shoulder of the elegant speaker.

MacManus, his mouth open, was smothered down one side of his dress suit in white paint. It turned his red carnation white and made his face more crimson. Roy had seen the Dodger owner angry on the field, but never like this. Sputtering and shaking paint over everyone near him, he turned with upraised fists ready to commit mayhem.

The big painter on the top of the ladder was not at all distressed. He stood surveying the damage. Then suddenly he removed his cap pulled down over his ears.

"How ar'ya, boss?" he said.

It was Razzle. On the other ladder, equally cool and imperturbable, was Harry Street.

15

Shoot!" remarked Rats Doyle in a disgusted tone. "They oughta told us about this here banquet. What kind of a way is that to run things?"

The whole squad was in a big bus. On the front of the bus was a sign: BROOKLYN BASEBALL CLUB. For the last game of all Dave had ordered them to meet early at the hotel and come to the park together.

"Shoot!" grumbled Rats. "Shoot! What kinda way is that to . . ." Rats indicated the majority opinion. Most of them felt as if a dirty trick had been played on them. Why weren't they told about the cars? No one likes to miss a good din-

ner, not to mention a gold wristwatch, a Ford
V8, and MacManus drowned in white paint. Up
and down the big bus ran the same query. Why
hadn't they been told?

There was another question those who missed
the party wanted answered.

"Was the boss sore?"

"Was he sore, Jerry?"

"Was he sore! I'll say!"

"What'd he do to Raz?"

"Hey, Razzle, bet you won't get a contract for
next season."

"If Leonard'll only put me in this afternoon
and I win that game, I'll get a contract all right.
And I'm gonna win, if he sends me in, too."

"Atta boy, Raz. But was he sore, was he?"

"You bet your life he was sore." Jerry Strong
spoke up. "Believe me, he was plenty sore at
first. Why, he like to go after Raz with his fists
up, didn't he, Roy?"

"He sure did. I didn't see much of what happened after the accident. I got out in the confusion. Boy, was I tired! I sneaked back to the
hotel and went to bed."

"Sore! Mac sore?" Fat Stuff had stayed to the
end, to see Razzle and Harry and Karl Case offi-
cially presented with new cars. "Say, first-off he

like to crown Raz, sure enough. Then he found
out it was all in fun, an' the paint wasn't paint at
all but just a little weak solution of whitewash
that would come right out. So he cooled down
and shook hands all round."

"Yeah, well, what could he do, with a couple
of sportswriters there and half of Brooklyn
watching him? But he was plenty sore at first.
Seemed like he'd slap a big fat fine on all of 'em.
Then he calmed down. He couldn't do anything
but take it in front of all that crowd there."

"He sure was sore though, at first."

"Say, know what happened to me when I got
back to the hotel last night?" The Kid was full of
a strange adventure. "I climb into bed, and I'm
sleeping there, and all of a sudden the phone
rings." No one was interested in his story. At the
other end of the bus a wordy argument was raging.

"Naw, let's give him a full one."

"Give who a full share? Who?" Heads went
together across the narrow aisle of the car.

"How 'bout Chiselbeak then?"

"Oh, a full one for old Chisel, I say."

"Me, too." The bus jounced round a corner.
"Hey, there, driver, watch yerself. We gotta bat
against Miller this afternoon." The underlying

thought in every mind. Miller! And that boy hot as a firecracker in his last game.

"Yeah, I think Chisel oughta have a full share."

"And a half share for the Doc?"

"The Doc? No, if Chisel gets a full share . . ."

"Say, you guys, quit that, will ya?" Old Fat Stuff reproved the younger members of the squad. "Don't you know it's bad luck dividing the shares before they're won. You boys are a bunch of saps."

Silence over the bus for a minute. Roy seized the chance to jump in with his amazing experience. "Know what happened? I climb into bed, and I'm almost asleep, and the telephone rings. 'Hullo. This Roy Tucker?' I'm pretty sleepy, so I say, 'Uhuh.' 'Okay,' says the voice. 'Well, we got a boy.' 'You gotta what?' 'We gotta boy, and I want you to come right down and help celebrate.' 'Aw, go to bed,' I say to this nut. 'Go to bed; it's almost midnight and I gotta have some sleep. Why, I'm batting against Miller tomorrow.' 'Nope,' he says. 'Nosir. You're coming out and help me celebrate. My wife's a great fan, too. And we gotta boy.' I had to tell the girl on the desk not to ring our room any more!"

"Yeah. That's nothing. In these Series a man

can't answer the telephone, he can't open the
door of his room, he can't sit quiet-like in a
hotel lobby, he can't do nothing."

"Know what I'm gonna do when this is over?
I'm gonna shut myself in a room and rest, all
alone. After a season of baseball with crowds
and more crowds day after day, a fellow feels
like goin' off and sitting down alone."

"Me, too. Hey, Fat Stuff, what you doing after
this is over?"

"I'm goin' hunting with Raz up in Wisconsin.
What about you?"

"Me? I'll spend a week up home with the folks
and then come back and play some golf a while.
What you doin', Roy?"

"I'm goin' fishin' for a while. All alone, too."

The bus jounced round a corner. "Say, what's
the matter with Red Allen? He looks as if he
hadn't had a shave for a week."

"That's the point. Seems he didn't shave in
Cleveland the day we were behind, and he's
been scared to shave ever since for fear we'd
lose. That's what eats him. He couldn't go to the
dinner last night 'cause he wasn't shaved, and
misses a new car all on account of it. He sure is
sick about missing that car."

"Well, I shaved this morning. And I shaved

myself, too," said Razzle. "First I tried to get me a shave in the hotel barbershop, and like to bust that barber's face in. While he's tucking the towel under my chin, he turns to his buddy in the next chair and cracks, 'If you ask me, that game yesterday was fixed, so's they can play it out today for a big gate.' "

Protests rose up and down the creaking bus.

"Why, the big bum!"

"Don't he know the players haven't any share in the gate after the fourth game?"

"What'd you do, Raz?"

"What'd I do? I ripped that towel offa my neck and jumped out of the chair and gave him a piece of my mind. 'I ought to flatten your nose for that one,' I told him. Then I beat it and went back to the room and shaved myself. I guess he's still wondering who the blazes I was."

"He must have found out soon enough if he didn't know then. Me, I want to win for old Dave Leonard."

"Same here."

"Me, too."

"Say, I'll break a leg for that old man."

"Okay, boys, le's win out there this afternoon for Dave."

"Yeah. We'll grab this off for Leonard."

Suddenly there was a shout of joy from the front of the bus. Street and McCaffrey sitting by the driver rose in their seats, pointing across the avenue where a big truck was passing them. It was a truckload of barrels. To pass a load of hay before a game was bad luck. To pass a load of barrels was the best luck possible.

The whole bus rose, staring after the truck and yelling. Oh, boy, what a break! They yelled and shouted as the ballpark came into sight. A load of barrels; just before facing Miller, too.

How could they know the truck had been planted on that avenue at that exact moment by Dave Leonard?

16

This was different!

It was the same room, the same scene, the same faces. Yet terribly different, too. In the corner were the black equipment trunks with BROOKLYN BASEBALL CLUB painted in red on the sides. There were the bats as usual slung on top of the green lockers, the shirts with their big numbers in blue hanging from wire hangers inside. There were Harry and Fat Stuff and Karl and Swanny and Rats and Jerry and the rest, all sitting about in various stages of undress. As usual Chiselbeak wound through the group, taking watches and money for the valuables trunk.

In short, the same scene that took place before every game.

But this was different! There was a different atmosphere in the room. No one was reading Casey's column. Babe Stansworth had thrown away his crossword puzzle, and no card game was in progress. The usual gang playing rummy in front of Karl's locker was missing, and the kibitzers who always hung over their shoulders were scattered. The room was oddly quiet. No jokes or wisecracks resounded; no one called to ask Razzle whether he had a date with his girl that evening. In fact, Raz was invisible. The team just sat. They sat solemnly on benches or stools by their lockers, pulling on their clothes, silent and subdued. This was different!

That first afternoon the Kid had felt everything depended on their meeting. Now he realized how much really hung on this last meeting of all. And on the game to come. For Dave Leonard it meant a new contract and a job in the years ahead. A fat contract, too; that MacManus was a fast gent with a dollar. The same for Fat Stuff and Rats Doyle and all the older players. Under a new manager they'd be traded to Buffalo or Montreal. No room for sentiment in baseball. Baseball is a business.

For each man on the squad, even for Chisel-beak and the Doc, that meeting or the game to follow might mean the difference between $6,400 and $4,400. For Razzle and himself and one or two others who had received commercial offers during the week, it would mean twice that much. If they won; if he batted .325. If he could only control his nerves and hit Miller. No wonder the room was quiet. Every man was thinking of what hung on that afternoon ahead.

He peeled off his clothes, put on a pair of shower sandals, and sat there, thinking. Old Chisel passed, apparently the same as ever; but impressed, in spite of all he could do to prevent it showing, by the seriousness of the moment. The Kid handed Chisel his new gold wristwatch and his money for the valuables trunk. Then he rose and went over to the alcove where the Doc's table stood. The Doc in white pants and a white undershirt was rubbing olive oil into Harry's back to prevent colds. Harry climbed off the table, and without a word Roy stretched out while the Doc anointed him. Then he went back, pausing at the entrance to Dave's little room. Dave was being strapped in a corset of tape over his back and thighs, with more tape around his legs. It was not a pretty sight. He turned. On the bulletin board were a dozen wires of good luck that had been pinned there by Chisel.

"TELL THE BOYS WE HERE ARE BACKING THEM EVERY MINUTE TO WIN THE SERIES AND WE LOOK FORWARD TO YOUR RETURN TO FLORIDA NEXT WINTER. CLEARWATER TOURIST BUREAU."

From the town where they held spring training. He glanced at several other telegrams, realizing that he was hardly reading them. So back to his locker where he resumed dressing.

For the last time he put on his sliding trunks and then sat down and pulled on his sweat socks and the outer socks over the sweat socks. Next he yanked at the long woolen undershirt which almost reached his knees. Then the baseball shirt with the big blue 34 on the back. Finally his trousers. Last of all he loosened his shoe-laces but did not put on the shoes.

"Meeting in five minutes, boys." Charlie Draper passed briskly through the room. This was usually the signal for the various groups to break up, for the card game to end. That morning there were no chattering groups and no card games.

Doggone, his shirt felt heavy. Outside the sun

was shining. So he peeled off his outer shirt and the heavy woolen undershirt, and replaced it by a light one without sleeves. Then he leaned over and tugged at his shoes. Still he didn't lace them. As a rule he kept them unlaced until the meeting was over.

Two thousand! Two thousand and a lot more hangs on this ball game. Now if only Raz pitches a good game. He will, though. The Kid recollected the times Razzle had pulled them from behind during the season. Razzle's a clutch pitcher. So it all depends on can we hit Miller. Can I hit him? That first time was no test. He really hadn't hit Miller since the beaning. The beaning! Ten days ago. Only ten days as you counted time. But sixty years in actual space. Sixty years with every minute that continual bong-bong-bong. Yep, it depended on today. On this afternoon, on how he made out against Miller. On whether or not he was scared. A feeling came over him. He didn't want to bat against Miller. He must be scared.

Forget it. Here comes Dave.

His toothpick in his mouth, as casual as ever, the old catcher entered the room followed by Draper, Cassidy, and Mike Sweeney, his brain trust. Draper had the big leather ball bag in his hand, Cassidy swung a bat, Dave walked stiffly.

"Now, boys." Silence, deeper than usual, settled over the room. Everyone sat up. Dave looked them over. A manager has to know all the men on the team, not five or six but everyone. He did know them; those who were a little numb, those who were tightened up, those who were tired mentally by the strain of coming from behind to win the last two games.

"Now, boys. Le's go out there and hustle this afternoon. We're all going home tonight, so what say we try and have some fun?" They glanced up at his casual tone. The toothpick waggling in his mouth showed his nerves to those who knew him; but few noticed its significance. To them Dave seemed loose and free, the same as ever. Yet more depended on it for him than any of them.

"Remember, there's nothing to worry about. We've come from behind, we showed we could do it and we've done it again. Others have won three straight in the Series; the Tigers in nineteen and thirty-five, for instance. If they can, you can. Once we get to Miller, it's in the bag. Those lads are just as tired as you are, and after yesterday's game they'll be ready to have the jitters today the first time the breaks don't go their way.

"You men have all hit against Miller before, and I b'lieve you'll do better this afternoon. He beat us in Cleveland, but he sure had luck that day. Don't forget; he has a very, very sneaky low pitch. If you swing at that low pitch he'll fool you every time."

The Kid tried to listen but he was hardly understanding the words. He was holding a meeting with himself. If I only don't put my foot in the bucket. If only I'm not scared . . .

". . . What say we pitch different to old Gardiner? You notice he's been hitting that first ball pretty reg'lar, and he's hitting, too. I b'lieve we can slow up to Hammy more. Jim Dennis of the Senators tells me their pitchers always feed him slow balls. Remember, Miller breaks his fast ball down and away from you right-hand hitters, and he tries to crack it straight down on you left-hand hitters. Watch this. That hit-and-run brought us good luck. We'll keep it up. Look out for it. Well . . . anyone got anything to ask before we go out there?"

Roy heard his voice, queer and croaky. Faces turned toward him. "Say . . . say, I'd like to know when there's a pitch-out. So's I can back up first, see? That throw of yours yesterday, Dave, like to catch me flatfooted."

"Okay, Harry; you let Roy know. No, wait a minute. Red, you let him know, hey? Any time Red slaps the calf of his left leg, a pitch-out is on. D'you get that, Roy? Get it? Okay. All right now, boys, go out there and take 'em.

"Hey, there. . . ." Dave stared over the heads of the group at the back of the room as if he had seen a ghost. Actually he had seen one. It was Razzle, his face completely whitened with thick face powder.

"Hey, there, Raz, what's the matter with you?"

"You told Casey yesterday you'd pitch the man who was the whitest, didn't ya? Well, look at me!"

The crowd roared. Dave joined in the laughter. The tension was broken as Dave turned and tossed him the ball. The room broke up in confusion.

"All right, gang, le's go. . . ."

"Yeah, le's win this one. For Leonard."

"Whoops, le's take this one for Dave."

"For Dave, sure, we'll win the one that counts for Leonard."

"For Dave . . . for Leonard . . . okay, for old Dave then." Clack-clack, clackety-clack their spikes sounded on the concrete runway to the field.

17

D ave stepped onto the windswept park in the crisp sunshine. His gaze went first to the flags in center field. The flags were out straight. Fine! That meant the wind was coming in. It would hold back the drives of the Indian power hitters and help his own fielders. So far, so good.

There seemed to be more reporters, photographers, radio men, and camp followers on the field back of the plate than on the first day, and the crowd milling around seemed larger than ever. Yet the stands were deserted. Roy, waiting to take his raps, remarked this to Rats Doyle.

"Isn't much of a crowd. Considering it's the seventh and everything."

"Last game," explained the old timer. "They always have trouble selling out this one. Folks are afraid they'll have trouble getting tickets and don't come out." He stepped to the plate, while a voice sounded at the Kid's elbow.

"Will you, please . . . for an old ballplayer?" A score card was shoved in his hand, with a pencil. He glanced curiously at the man to see what he himself would be like in twenty years, and scrawled his name. "Thanks," said the old fellow, moving away. Others noticed this, and immediately a messenger boy came up with a program. Then he was surrounded. They handed him baseballs, programs, score cards, scratch pads, and leather-covered autograph books. For some time he stood signing, his bat under his arm. Then it was his turn, and he broke away to go to the plate. The plate itself had been newly painted. It was fresh and white and there were clean neat spike-marks in the clay.

When he returned to the dugout waving his bat, he found Harry sitting on top of the bench, his feet on the board seat below, laughing at a girl who was taking his picture from outside.

"Yes, ma'am, go right ahead and break your machine if you want to." The old pop-off. Harry was loose; anyone could see he was loose. Several sportswriters climbed down inside.

"H'ya, Sandy."

"Hullo there, Rex."

"Good morning, Tommy." A couple more followed. They surrounded the Kid on the bench, asking questions.

"How you feel, Roy?"

"Me? I'm all right."

"Feel any different?"

"No. 'Course I don't feel different." Yet inside he realized he did feel different. Except for the bunting over the upper and lower tiers and the flags and the band, the Series was much like an ordinary game. Not the last one, with all that money hanging on it. You felt different, no matter what anyone said. Before the dugout he noticed Razzle, also encircled by a group of reporters. Then the big pitcher broke away, took his glove from his hip pocket, and walked out onto the field. The Kid understood. He wanted to be alone, to get away from foolish questions, autograph collectors, photographers, and sportswriters.

From his seat the Kid could look into the

Cleveland dugout across the way. Baker sitting on the step watching the Dodger hitters was apparently as unconcerned as Dave, who just then was signing for a telegram with a casual air, talking to Casey all the while. He opened the telegram and passed it down the bench. An enormous affair, the telegram when unfolded was almost six feet long.

"WE HERE IN CLEARWATER TAKE THIS MEANS OF WISHING YOU LUCK TODAY."

There were hundreds of signatures. A group gathered round, and several photographers knelt outside the dugout, snapping Harry and Rats together glancing over the names.

"CLANG-CLANG-CLANG" went the bell. Fat Stuff came into the dugout, swinging his bat and grumbling. "Twenty years it's been like that. I go up to bat and what happens? The bell rings." With disgust he shoved his bat into its slot in the bat rack, murmuring to himself, "Why shouldn't pitchers have a crack at the ball once in a while?"

The rest of the team returned, slapping their bats into place, knocking the dirt from their spikes on the stone step of the dugout. Then spreading themselves on the seat, they watched the Indians full of fire and pepper take the field.

Glancing down the bench Roy could tell the ones who were tight by the way they sat, chins cupped in their hands, staring at the figures in the field. And those who were loose, too, like Harry with his arms over the back of the bench, relaxed and talking with Casey. "We're sure gonna tie into 'em today. . . ." A few were concentrated on their rivals lining out drives at the plate; others were just dreaming. But all were thinking the same thing: can we hit Gene Miller?

From above them came the sounds and cries of the ballpark. ". . . can't tell the players without a score card . . . get 'em red-hot . . . they're red-hot . . . peanuts and popcorn . . . peanuts and popcorn . . . who's next . . . anybody else wanna cold drink . . . anyone else . . . only twenty-five cents . . . score cards . . ."

Then a voice came over the loudspeaker and a sudden sharp yell greeted the words:

"For Brooklyn, No. 14 . . . Nugent. . . ."

The fans were on edge. Miller against Nugent. A struggle of giants, with fifty thousand dollars depending on every inning, every pitch, every play.

Then came that moment which took place before every game, a moment usually unperceived by the crowd. But Roy, realizing its significance, could never see it without a catch in his throat. A lonely group of half a dozen players—pitchers and catchers—detached themselves from the dugout and walked slowly across the field. Relief men going to the bullpen. Just in case.

The band struck up "The Star-Spangled Banner" and everyone rose on the bench, cap in hand. The last notes died away and an outburst of chatter went up and down the line; their way of trying to allay their tension as the big moment drew near. Together they boiled out of the dugout. In the movement forward, the Kid jostled sleeves with Ed and Swanny on each side. That friendly touch gave him courage. Anyhow the Dodgers were a team, they were a unit, all in it together.

He raced toward right. The stands rose as he passed. Coming into his position he faced the bleachers in deep right center where the Knot Hole Gang was sitting. Now they were on their feet, shouting through their hands, yelling encouragement. He could even distinguish voices in the roar.

"Go get 'em, Roy. . . ."

"You can do it, Tuck. . . ."

"Give us one them homers, Roy. . . ."

"Atta boy, Kid. . . ."

They knew him. And he knew them. Through those terrible periods of July and August they had stayed behind the team; winning or losing, in rain, cold, wind, heat, they were always there. Here they were for the last game of all, his friends, sticking with him to the very end.

Say, it was swell to play in Brooklyn. He wouldn't want to play anywhere else. They knew him, this gang, and he knew them. Nearing his position, he waved and the crowd howled with delight.

A guy was lucky to be able to play ball for a crowd like that. With a manager like Dave Leonard behind you.

18

Mc Clusky swung hard and missed the ball. Instead of stepping from the box and rubbing his hands on his uniform as he usually did whenever he swung from his ears, he walked ten feet away and scooped up a handful of dirt. Roy, watching closely, knew immediately what this meant. McClusky was nervous. The Indian batters were tight, too.

A minute later they were coming in to the dugout. Nearing first, the Kid saw Razzle go through his customary pantomime. As he neared the foul line on his way from the box to the bench the big pitcher tossed his glove some distance ahead. It fell toward the dugout, and on getting to it he leaned over and turned the glove upside down. Then he walked in to the bench.

"Just get me one run, gang, that's all. One run, that's all I ask; one run."

Shoot! That's no good. The bench leaned back together in resignation as Red Allen flied to Rock.

"Now then, Roy, what say we go places. . . ."

"Okay, Kid, you can do it. . . ."

"Unbutton your shirt up there, Roy. . . . "

He stepped to the plate. In the box the big pitcher stood motionless on the rubber, arms on his hips, legs apart, looking inquiringly at McCormick. All the friendly look had vanished. In its place was an ugly grin, and with that tooth missing in front he seemed to Roy the meanest man he ever faced. The bong-bong-bong in the Kid's head sounded louder than ever while the pitcher shook off his catcher and then, nodding, went into his wind-up. Roy connected with a hook on the first pitch and started for first as if he were running a hundred yard dash. Close; but the ball was ahead of him. Returning to the dugout he felt a tremendous sense of relief, almost light and happy. It might be three innings before he'd have to bat again.

With both pitchers throwing airtight ball, the innings went by rapidly and it hardly seemed any time before they were swarming back into the dugout at the end of the third, the score still nothing to nothing.

Then in the fourth inning things happened. The Kid realized as he had so often before that every situation in baseball was different and that new situations arose every day. The top of the Cleveland batting order was up, with Lanahan at bat. He smacked a hard drive near first for which Red ran desperately. He stabbed at it and missed. Roy was waiting and froze the ball, but Lanahan was safe on first.

Raz went back to the mound and he and Dave started to work on McClusky with care. The Kid dug the dirt from his spikes, set himself ready to move, flexed his arm . . .

An easy out. A grounder. A doubleplay ball. In fact *the* perfect doubleplay ball, a rolling grounder to Harry, right where he liked it on his throwing side. Directly the ball was hit Roy broke in toward second, although Harry was never known to mess up the throw from any position. Nor did he; the throw was chest high and perfect. With desperation Lanahan slid into second. Then realizing he was beaten, he dug his spikes into Ed's left leg, bowling him over before he could snap the ball to first. It dribbled dangerously along the dirt toward the grass in right field.

Instantly the situation changed. The Cleveland coaches on the base lines became dancing figures, on their toes yelling. The stands rose shrieking. The whole diamond was alive with shouts and the figures of racing men, as Lanahan jumped up and dashed for third while McClusky turning first darted for second. This might well be the game, the fifty thousand dollar break, the whole thing. The two runners tore for the forward bases as the ball bounded aimlessly.

Roy, charging in, saw Lanahan's trick, saw the loose ball, and bore down with everything he had. There was still a chance, a good chance. He neared the ball lying motionless on the grass.

"Third . . . third . . . hurry up . . . take yer time . . . third . . . Roy. . . ."

Timing his stride exactly, he scooped the ball up with his bare hand while still on the run and, raging inside, rifled it into third all in the same motion. Jerry, the old reliable, was waiting. He whanged the ball on Lanahan and shot it back to second. McClusky had overslid the bag and before he could scramble to safety Ed had completed the double play.

A roar rose all round the diamond as in the flash of a few seconds the situation shifted from confidence to disaster and back again to confidence. Heads-up ball had saved them momentarily. A minute later they trooped back to the dugout, panting, hot, weary. No wonder Ed dropped that ball. He showed an ugly gash down the side of his leg and even his shoe was so cut and ripped as to be unwearable. The team gathered round as the Doc patched him up with tape and brought out another shoe. Then they settled back. Dave leaned down the bench approvingly.

"That's picking them up, there, Roy. Did me good to see you go for that ball."

"Boy, you really can throw that old apple," said Jerry. "Like to burn my hands offa me."

He felt encouraged by their words which gave him strength and confidence. "Okay, Razzle, we'll go get you your run this inning; just you see if we don't."

Allen up, Tucker in the hole. Dave called down the bench to the Kid as he pulled his bat from the slot.

"Now, Roy, go get me a single. Just a single, will ya?"

"Only one run, that's all I ask, only one run, Tuck old kid." By gosh they'd get it, too. This was the inning.

On one knee in the circle, now almost enshadowed, he watched Red take the first one, swing hard at a hook, and then crack the next pitch on the nose.

"IT'S A HIT! A HIT! OH, BOY! IT'S A HIT!"

A hit it was, the first real clean hit of the game, a scorching drive which Gordon fielded well to hold Red from going to second. The Kid watched anxiously but Cassidy held him at first.

He stepped to the plate, determined to forget the bonging in his head, the swoosh of Miller's fast one close in, the nearness of the big man in the box. Miller looked as diabolical as ever on that mound. Once again he shook off his catcher. Roy took the signal and watched one go past, right across. Then expecting a fast ball, he hit. It was a slow grounder, a grass cutter beyond Hammy and far to the left of Gardiner. But that old man was fast just the same, he was going hard, and Roy dug in, giving everything he had, straining as if the game itself depended on his speed. A burst of noise came from the stands as he flashed past the bag. Safe!

There! That would spark 'em. That would start the boys below him rolling. Two hits in succession off the great Miller. Panting and heaving from his effort, he stood on first watching the signals.

Swanny at the plate rubbed his uniform, thinking he'd take the first one. Ball. Then Swanny made a gesture which left Roy puzzled. This was important. Mustn't make any mistake, because the way the two pitchers were going this inning might decide the whole game. So he leaned over and tied his shoe to indicate that he had missed the signal. Charlie Draper back of third base hitched his belt. Roy, one foot on the bag, hitched his to show he understood. A hit-and-run on the third pitch.

"Strrrike . . . " growled old Stubblebeard back of the plate. One and one. Here was the pay-off pitch. Now for it. There . . . there. . . .

Swanny swung a trifle late and only got a piece of the ball. The result was a nicely hopping roller between first and second. Gardiner, back on the grass, came forward a few feet and instantly the Kid saw what was coming: the quick throw to second, the one to first to nab

Swanny, the doubleplay for which the two old timers were famous, which they had made thousands of times in their baseball career. The Dodger rally would be killed at the start.

Nearer, nearer came the ball. With an extra burst of speed he dived at it and let the ball catch him full on the thigh. It caromed off and bounded away. Gardiner ran to retrieve the ball, but Swanny was automatically safe at first and Red was still securely perched on second, having checked his dive for third when he saw the play.

He came back to the bench. One down, but there was no doubleplay. Or maybe he should have done what Lanahan had done in the same situation. "Was that the right play there, Dave, or should I have slid into Lanny to break it up?"

"Just right, Roy. You did the smart thing. Now boys, one down."

Beyond him on the bench sat Razzle, pulling at his cap and repeating half to himself, "Only one run, boys, give me one run. That's all I ask, one run."

"One down. Only one down," shouted the coaches, holding up a finger. From the bleachers in right came the roar of his gang pleading for a hit.

Karl Case tried hard to respond. His best effort was a pop-up to Lanahan. Two down. Run on anything. Now, Harry, it's up to you, old timer. The coaches were yelling, the stands yowling for a hit. Harry's effort wasn't much. A looping Lena that Hammy couldn't quite reach back of first. Gordon running full tilt came racing in, his glove outstretched. He reached out, missed, and the ball fell safe in the field. Red racing hard came across with Razzle's run. The Dodgers were in the lead at last.

Jerry Strong, the next man up, struck out with Swanny stranded on third. The inning was over but they had the fifty thousand dollar run. They'd given Razzle the run he asked for. Now they only had to protect that lead.

Easy and loose, Roy trotted out to the field, passing Gordon, hot, panting, angry.

"Boy, were you lucky on that one! Six inches closer and I'd had it."

"Yeah, maybe, Bruce. Well, class'll tell," responded the Kid lightheartedly. Who said we were licked? As Casey put it, there's no quit in the Dodgers.

Ahead of him the boys in the bleachers were

on their feet, yelling. They yelled and yelled insistently, so he yanked at his cap. They yelled louder. Say, with a gang like that back of you every minute, with a manager like old Dave at the plate, no wonder they'd come from behind to win.

19

For almost the first time since the second game the pressure was on the Indians. This the Dodgers realized. One saw it in their attitude, in their confident manner, in the loud and breezy crackle around the infield, in Karl's sharp tones from left center, in Swanny's deep boom, encouraging, supporting. While all the time Raz towered on the mound, master of the situation.

Now the pressure was off the Dodgers. They had that vital, precious run. It was a question of which pitcher would crack first. Inning after inning passed. The shadows slowly lengthened to cover more and more of the diamond.

All over the stands the fans rose to slip on over-coats. And every minute victory came closer and closer.

They came into the seventh with only nine more outs to get; only nine men between them and victory. It was beautiful to watch Raz and Dave despite their fatigue go to work on Gordon. To see them together in harmony gave the Kid added courage. We'll get this man for you, Raz. Let him hit it. First the batter swung at a fast one. Then he watched a ball, and on the third swung again from his ears. The crowd jeered. He fouled an outside pitch. Raz had him. Raz was ahead of the batters. The man at the plate swung, swung viciously, missing a mean one close to his body. First man. Only eight to go.

The ball snapped briskly round the infield and was finally thrown to Harry. Every team has one man who feeds the ball to the pitcher. On the Dodgers it was Street.

That's pitching, Raz old boy, old kid. That's chucking, that is. Why, Bruce like to swing himself clean into his dugout on that-there pitch. Say, is Raz a pitcher! Six, nope, five strikeouts so far. He's a clutch pitcher, old Raz is. Now for McCormick. Mac is just a bread-and-butter player at bat.

"Okay, Raz old boy, let him hit."

Raz smoothed the dirt before the rubber, hitched his shirt, raised his arms and stood watching Dave with care. Getting the sign he nodded, looked round, and went to work. Mac swung with all his strength. The ball popped into Dave's mitt and again the chatter rose from the diamond. Boy, if he'd hit that one he'd have plunked it over the fence. Anxiously the Kid backed up a few yards. He's hitting hard. He sure is trying. But Raz is too good for him.

Look out! From deep right Roy saw Mac suddenly set his feet and dump a perfect bunt along the third base line. Jerry deep on the grass was caught unexpectedly on his heels. Charging in fast, he stabbed at the ball with one hand, missed it, and the hit went for a single. Immediately a burst of noise came from the Indian dugout. With reluctance the Kid admitted to himself the smartness of the play. They swing from their ears and set us up for a hard hit ball, then they bunt one. That's smart baseball. That's crossing us up, all right.

The Indians came to the step of their dugout, shouting. The bench was all in shadow; so was most of the infield as Roy stood wondering whether Baker would throw in a pinch hitter for big Miller. Then Miller, muffled up in a sweater, came to the plate. He remembered that Miller was not a bad hitter. He wasn't any slouch at the bat.

Supremely confident of a Dodger victory, the crowd could afford to be generous and gave him a big hand. The Cleveland star had pitched a grand game, his third in the Series, holding them down to one clean hit in six innings. Raz went to work with care. The pressure was on the batter but that old right field fence beckoned and a single poor throw could mean disaster. He fed Miller a couple of teasing pitches. Gene was not tempted. He was no two o'clock hitter. Then Raz sneaked over a strike. 2 and 1.

The next ball Miller hit, hit hard. It went on a line toward third. Jerry with a lunge reached it, knocked it down, and deflected its movement. The ball rolled toward the stands while the diamond dissolved in movement. Jerry hustled over for it inside the foul line, Karl dashed in vainly from left, McCormick rounded second, Harry ran to cover third, and Miller lumbered past first. The stands rose, watching anxiously as Jerry pursued the bounding ball. Now Mac was nearing third, streaking for home, Miller almost at second. Too late to save the run.

"Third, Jerry, take yer time . . . hurry up. . . ." The tieing run was across; the teams were even again.

Then without any cause, without any rhyme or reason, the Dodger defense faltered. The strain suddenly told. That infield which had played faultless ball for so many games all at once crumpled and cracked. An easy bounder of Lanny's drew a bad throw from Harry who never made bad throws. It took Red off the bag long enough to plant runners on first and second. Now the fifty thousand dollars really hung on every single pitch. The noise of the dugouts lessened, the roar of the stands died away as the shadows lengthened across the field. Quiet hung about the diamond while Raz hitched his belt, stuffed in his shirt, and taking his glove from under his armpit stepped to the rubber.

McClusky smacked the first pitch. A line drive between first and second, the kind of a hit Ed ordinarily would have had in his pocket. He ran over, failed to touch it, and the ball went through. Roy saw it coming, bouncing toward him along the ground, and picking up the dribbling sphere he turned and threw to second. Instantly he realized his error. He should have thrown home. They could have nabbed Gene

Miller who was tearing for the plate. Or anyhow held him at third.

Miller took over the second run and a minute later when Gardiner flied deep to Karl, Lanny came across with the third. Rock ended the inning by popping to Harry and three runs had been scored. Three to one. There was little to say after an inning like that, and most of them were far too numb to talk. Imagine, throwing a game away on easy chances.

Holy suffering Codfish, thought Roy, if only I hadn't booted that one, we'd only be one run behind. I threw it away on that bonehead play. Usually my throwing instincts are good, too; usually I make the right play. Well, the boys won't hold it against me. All they ask is, a man should hustle. I'll hustle now. See if I don't.

But like the rest, in his heart he knew they were up against it. That's baseball. One bad inning and bang goes fifty thousand dollars. Six innings of first class pitching, then a couple of simple mistakes and the game is lost. One moment you have a world's championship in your hands. Then next you're two runs behind.

"Who's up? Karl? Okay, Case old boy, give us a hit. Start things moving, will ya?"

But that three-run inning had given confidence to the Indians and strengthened their worn and haggard pitcher. They were relaxed and loose behind Miller, and he was loose, too, for when a pitcher is hitting well you can be sure he hasn't any nerves. Gardiner knocked down a drive to nip Karl by inches at first. Harry popped to McCormick. Jerry tried hard with no luck, and Lanahan tagged his liner.

Start of the eighth. The diamond and most of the outfield was deep in shadow, giving every Dodger a feeling of desperation as he walked to his position. Like a menace of approaching doom those lengthening shadows foretold disaster . . . unless they got two runs. Two runs anyway; we'll settle for two runs but we really need three. Two runs for Dave, fellas, we gotta grab us off two runs for Leonard. Behind the plate the old catcher went wearily into his crouch. Ed nailed Hammy at first. Then Dave waved the Kid toward right for Painter, always a dangerous man. The batter smacked a wicked liner at Roy. In fact he stood to take it without even moving his feet. Dave knew the hitters all right, Dave sure knew the batters. Raz then struck out Gordon. Say, he hasn't given up, he's really bearing down as much as ever, old Razzle is. What a money player. Hot, sweating, anxious, they trooped into the dugout for the end of the eighth.

Ed Davis, the first man up, flied out to center field.

Dave had unbuckled his shin guards and taken his bat from the boy.

"Okay, Dave, here's where we pick you up."

"Le's get 'em back, Dave, and more, too."

The Kid took a drink of water and squeezed in beside Raz, who was pulling on a sweater.

"How you feel, Raz?"

Razzle rubbed his right leg. "The old pusher's kinda tired. If only we can pick up a couple of runs." His eyes were on Dave walking to the plate. Roy followed his gaze, noticing how sore and stiff the catcher was. He even limped slightly as he went into the batter's box. And we let him down, me, and Harry, and Ed, and Strong. We let him down. Now it's up to us to come through for him. We gotta come through for Dave.

A double! A clean one, sailing over third and falling safe inside the left foul line. Now we're off. Boy, is that old man a ballplayer! *Is* he there in the clutch! Raz is up. Raz, however, was sitting quietly on the bench. He's pulling Razzle. Yep, he's pulling him. The Babe is gonna bat.

A voice over the loudspeaker tried hard to outshout the crowd but lost the decision as big Stansworth, his taped thumb in evidence, came to the plate. The Babe was a favorite of the bleachers. His clumsy and familiar figure shuffling to bat drew heartening cheers round the dusk-covered field.

One down. Leonard on second, Stansworth at bat. By gosh! He won't . . . yes, he's passing him. That's not percentage ball. Guess Baker's playing a hunch here. It looked like it as the Cleveland catcher stepped to the side of the plate and received four wide ones in his mitt.

Stansworth trotted down to first, where he was immediately relieved by Roth as a runner. First and second, one down. A roar started in the bleachers. It began with the gang in right, spread to the stands in left, caught hold of the mob behind third, back of the plate, and rose, a loud, continuous shout. They shrieked, they pleaded for a hit as Red whacked his bat on the plate. Along the bench no one could sit still. The gang stood, clapping their hands, yelling at the batter. As he fouled one off they jumped out, watching the ball's curve into the stands. 1 and 1. An important pitch.

Now there, Red. Red's a good man in a tight

place. We're sure in a pinch. Coupla runs behind, and there they are on the bags, Dave and Paul Roth.

On one knee in the circle Roy watched with reluctant admiration as a fast one sizzled past Red's ear. No use talking, that baby is a pitcher. He can pitch. Now Red, powder that ball. A foul. Another foul high in the stands. And another. Atta boy, Red. That's the old stuff; wear him down; make him throw his heart out. Red's unselfish; he's a team player all right.

The next pitch was fast, low and outside. The catcher half stopped it, but somehow it got away and spun along the ground. Like a shot he pounced on it, but Dave, ever alert, was quicker still. With a desperate slide he came down the basepath head first, the last fifteen feet on his belly, catching the edge of the bag as Painter with the ball in his glove groped down for something to tag.

The stands rose yelling. There's a break. Leonard on third, Roth on second, only one out. Who said the Dodgers were quitters?

Almost the whole field was deep in shade as the big man in the box looked round at his outfield, nodded to his catcher, and stepped on the rubber. He smoothed the dirt with one foot, hitched up his pants, and glanced over his shoulder at second base. Then he threw. A ball. 3 and 2. Now Miller *was* on the spot.

He's got to put it over. Smack it, Red! Give us that hit for Dave. Give us one for Leonard, will ya?

IT'S A HIT. A HIT. The ball, struck well and cleanly, was high and deep. But the wind carried it back; that same wind which was to work against the Indian power hitters was ironically saving the day for them. Rock was there waiting under it as it fell. Dave dashed for home, straining. The fielder, however, made no attempt to catch him. Instead he threw into third to prevent Roth advancing beyond second.

The bat boy came up to take Red's bat. He had a towel in his hands. "Hey, there, boy, gimme that towel," said the Kid, wiping his hands. In the dugout they were all on the step, frantically yelling.

Now then. It's up to me. Here's a poke for old Dave. I'm not scared now. I'll sure punch that ball. If he's gonna bean me he's gonna bean me. I'll crack it, sure enough. Two out, but I'll hit one for Dave. This is for Leonard.

He stepped to the plate. One glance showed Miller's fatigue, his tired face under the cap, his

mouth open in an exhausted pant. The first ball
was low. Roy got a piece of the second and
fouled it off. Then that low one again, the
sneaker pitch.

Didn't fool me, did ya, mister? Gimme a good
one, boy, I sure want to hit it. Nope, wide. Not
that time.

McCormick returned the ball with a quick
wrist motion. Miller spun round and snapped it
to Lanahan. The old fox beat Roth to the bag at
second and the Dodgers were out. Still one run
behind.

Shucks! Roy hurled his bat on the plate with
all his force. There's a rookie for you. The kid
wasn't watching. That would never have happened to Karl or Swanny or me. Shoot! And
we're still one run behind.

20

Now who'll pitch? Now who'll Leonard throw in? Not Fat Stuff—he's washed up. Not McCaffrey—he pitched yesterday. Rats is a cousin for these birds.

Walking wearily to right, the Kid watched the activity in their bullpen. Two men were burning in quick last pitches. Then a tall figure came walking through the shadow across the field.

Not Rog Stinson. Yep, Roger Stinson. The freshman pitcher, the quiet kid who never said a word to anyone, the colt who had only seen a few months' play; who was trying to put the Columbus Red Birds in the first division only the summer before. The whole crowd was stunned. They listened in silence to the loudspeaker.

"Stinson, No. 22, pitching for Brooklyn." What a spot for a kid, although he had Dave there working with him and for him. Dave walked onto the diamond, met the boy, and put his arm round the rookie's shoulder. He said something to him as the team in the field chattered.

"Okay, Rog old boy. . . ."

"Le's go, there, Roger. . . ."

Roger burned in several pitches. What a spot! The start of the ninth, the field enveloped in shadow, the Dodgers one run behind, and McCormick, Miller, and old Lanny taking their raps. Boy, you'll either be a bum or a hero. One or the other, thought Roy, as he watched the two go to work, the kid fresh and cool from the bullpen, the old catcher sore and exhausted after two hours of struggle.

McCormick hit the second pitch. It rose in the air, high, high, and settled in Harry's glove. The crowd yelled. They were all behind the boy in the box. Miller took a strike, then smacked a hard one to the right of first. Red knocked it down and tossed it to Stinson. Racing in to cover up, Roy saw the pitcher wheel, get across to the bag, and grab the ball just as the runner flashed past. A cool customer, that boy. Dave was correct in placing confidence in him. Dave's judgment was good. They'd come through yet. They'd have to pull this one out for Dave.

Now for Lanny. Lanny's one tough baby. He's hit my way so I'll hafta watch close. The Kid clawed the dirt from his spikes, feeling an ache in his legs as he did so. Imagine how Dave must feel, sore and lame all over. The first pitch got away and rolled in front of the plate. Dave, too tired to reach over, kicked it back along the ground to the pitcher. That betrayed plainly enough how Dave felt.

Lanny hit. The ball was tagged, too. Roy playing toward center tore back, gauging its flight as he neared the stands. Closer he went, closer. Might get hurt; that didn't matter; he was going to risk injury to get the ball as all money players do. Over one shoulder he saw the stands, the fence of concrete and wire, then the ball high above descending. His cap fell off as he clutched at the wire with his right hand and pulled himself up as far as possible. Above his head his glove shot into the air . . . and there was the ball. He lost hold, tumbled down, rolled over on the turf, all the time clutching that ball.

They yelled. They yelled and yelled. They were still yelling when he came to the plate swinging the two bats a minute later. He threw away the big lead bat, weighted so that when you swung the real bat it seemed lighter and quickened your reflexes. They were still yelling when he stepped up, so he touched his cap. The field was ominously dim as late afternoon descended over the ballpark, covered the stands and the outfield, shrouded the diamond and the box and Miller wiping his face with his sleeve. It shrouded them all; Lanny there at short and old fox Gardiner at second, familiar faces by this time; Charlie Draper coaching behind third, and . . . yes . . . Dave. The manager himself had taken over the coaching box at first. Dave was standing there, pleading for a hit.

The Kid took one perfect strike, let Miller's sinker go past, fouled one, and had another ball. 2 and 2. Often he had heard Dave on the bench remark that you could usually slip a fast one by most batters at 2 and 2. Watching Miller carefully during the Series he had counted five times the big man threw a fast ball at 2 and 2, and only once a curve. So he set himself for the fast one.

It was fast, too, straight, and straight he caught it. Dave was urging him on as he passed first, and from third Charlie gave him the sign to slide. With everything he had he went in, low, hard, on Lanahan's ankles. The old timer had his legs well anchored, but the fierceness and rush of Roy's body upset him. He tottered, stumbled, fell, and the Kid was safe.

Lanny growled something as he picked himself up and limped back to his position. Roy leaned over and snatched a fistful of dirt in each hand so he would remember to keep his fists up when sliding. Now tempers were high, nerves rasped, everyone was on edge, and a man couldn't be too careful. The roar about the field increased, rose, fell, rose again as Swanson shuffled confidently to bat. In the stands the smoke of thousands of cigarettes made a kind of haze through the gathering dusk, and panting there on second Roy could see wisps of flame from lighted matches. The crowd was yelling furiously.

Nope, the Dodgers weren't licked yet. No sir! In the coaching box Dave clenched his fists at Swanny. Fight, fight, fight! Dave, who always said that the best manager was the man who did the least managing, was out there lifting them by his will power back into the game. Hauling them, pulling them along, making them hit, setting an example to every man on the team.

Come on now, Swanny. Roy took the signal. Swanson watched a low one. Then he laid a perfect bunt toward third. Painter dashing in thought it was rolling foul and stood watching it. By this time Roy was perched on third and could see the whole drama; the slow roller, the men gathering about it, Painter, Miller, Baker who ran out of the dugout, Draper, Lanahan, and Stubblebeard, the umpire. Then the ball trickled off into foul territory and came to a stop. All this Roy noticed. He noticed what the rest had missed. Lanahan, the old trickster who had run over from short, had quietly scraped a trench with his spikes directly in the path of the ball. As it neared third and caught the track it was deflected foul. Instantly the Kid ran up to Stubblebeard and Catfish Simpson, the third base umpire, standing over the ball with the others.

"Look! Hey, look here, Stubble . . . look . . . see what he did . . . see, this track here took the ball off the diamond . . . made it roll foul . . . he can't do that. . . ."

The fans back of third were roaring, also. Some of them had seen what everyone on the field except Roy had missed. Stubblebeard waved Swanson to first and Roy back to third. And nobody out.

Pandemonium. Anything goes now. Any kind of a scratch hit, Karl. Anything at all, old boy. Just a Texas Leaguer, a looping Lena, anything, yep, even a doubleplay ball. I'll get home on a doubleplay ball, I'll get home on any kind of a hit.

Karl caught the first pitch dead on the nose. By the sound Roy knew it had carry. On third he saw McClusky go back, hands up, head in the air. He stood, poised for the flight, ready to run as never in his life before. He ran. Beside the plate was McCormick, fists clenched in the air, watching the play which was to second base. Roy flashed across and into the arms of Dave.

Above, the stands shrieked and thundered. They howled, they yowled, they stamped and whistled. They called and catcalled at Miller. Now the score was tied. When he reached the dugout the entire team was on the step, arms outstretched. It was a sea of hands, and he had to shake every hand all the way up and down the bench before they'd let him get to the water cooler. 3 to 3.

The Dodgers were in there once more. They were back in the running. No wonder the bleachers boiled over in deep right, no wonder the bench was in turmoil, no wonder Whitehouse and the relief pitchers were croaky from shouting. What did it matter if Harry struck out and Ed Davis popped to Hammy, leaving Swanny and Jerry Strong on bases? The Dodgers had come back. They hadn't quit. They were in the race again.

When he took his position in the field, the stands, *his* stands, rose to greet him. He felt their loyalty and waved. They shrieked still louder and tossed score cards and rolled newspapers into the air. Their Tucker, their Kid, had come through with the tieing run.

First of the tenth. The flashes of lighted matches in the smoky gloom were plainer now than ever. It was getting late, for the game had lasted over two hours already. At the plate, Dave held up one clenched fist, turning slowly from left to right, waving it at Jerry and Karl, then at Harry and Swanson in deep center, then at Ed and Red and himself, pulling them up, onward, knitting them together as a team. The rookie in the box went to work. Roy was confident. This kid did so well last inning we don't have to worry. As long as Dave lasts we're set.

McClusky popped up on the second pitch. His mask on the ground, Dave turned, following the ball toward their dugout, his head in the air. Could he get to it . . . reach it . . . hold it? Yes. He was there, he hugged the ball. For just a second or two he stood puffing beside the bench, slapping the ball into his mitt. Roy couldn't hear the words but he knew the tune. Lemme know on those balls, boys, lemme know when I'm close to the bench . . .

Gardiner. At the 2 and 2 count he hit. But he swung late, and Harry sensing this started for second. The ball hopped over Roger's head into the hands of the alert shortstop. There, that's heads-up ball for you. Dashing behind first to cover up, Roy could see Harry on second take plenty of time and then rifle the ball to first like a bullet. As the Kid slowed down back of the foul line he saw Dave also hauling up behind first, haggard and exhausted. Gosh, what a trier, what a ballplayer that man is!

Rock. Dave waved him over. Way over. We'll nab Rock okay. He fouled one. Then he took a strike and fouled another, a high one, close to

the Dodger bench again. This time the whole
dugout was up yelling.

"You got it, Dave. . . ."

"Plenty of room, old timer. . . ."

"Ten feet, Dave. . . ."

"You got room, Dave. . . ." He gathered in
the ball. The side was out. And Leonard at bat.

No wonder the stands rose cheering. He
wouldn't touch his cap so they roared the louder.
Then he had to touch it. Give us another hit, old
timer; show us the way this time. He hit the ball
hard but Rock was under it. Dave pulled up at
first and took over the coach's box from Cassidy.

Roger's up. Rog isn't a bad hitter, either. Give
us a start there, Rog. Win your own game. Save
me a rap, Roger. The whole dugout was now on
the step, full of fight and pepper, shrieking
through cupped hands, pleading, yelling. Come
on now, Rog; just get to first. But old Miller had
something still left. He struck Rog out. Two
down and Red at bat.

Red took a vicious cut but it wasn't even close.
Roy stood yelling with the rest. C'mon on there,
Red, show him what the Dodgers can do. Two
out and one run to go. We'll get it, boys. We've
done it with two gone before this.

In the coaching box back of first Dave turned

toward the stands with uplifted arms. Give us some encouragement. Make some noise. Show these boys you're behind them. He knew also the effect that pandemonium was having on the Cleveland team. The field boiled over. On the Dodgers' bench and in the dugout no one could stay still. They flowed onto the step, out on the grass. Red hit a foul. As one man the team jumped to watch it curve and die away in the upper stands.

Then Red hit. It was a low line drive at Painter. The ball took its first bounce right by his feet, struck his glove and rolled behind him. He turned the wrong way and for just a second or two could not find the ball. Then he pounced on it and threw to first hurriedly. The throw was wide, and Red beat it to the bag.

There's our break. The Dodgers make the breaks. They fight for the breaks and get 'em. Now watch us move. The dugout was in an uproar. Deep in right field the fans, Roy's fans, were on their feet, shrieking at him, appealing for a hit. He felt their support and was confident of his ability to end the game. The chance never came. Miller, anxious not to give a ball he could hit, got himself in a hole. The last one was close, but the umpire waved Roy to first. Two out and two men on base. Swanny at bat. I know he'll come through, thought the Kid as he stood with one foot on the bag. He'll come through in the clutch, Swanny will. He's a team player, he never lets us down, he'll come through for us now.

In the dim dusk the Kid saw the ball rise, a high, hard hit swing off Miller's fast one. Gordon in right went back, hands up. A tough catch but he's a good player; if I can make 'em out there he can, too. Roy's friends in the bleachers were in a frenzy. As he neared second the Kid saw the stands as a queer dissolving, squirming mass. Gordon stood strangely motionless by the wire watching the ball vanish in the confusion above.

You fought, you struggled. You pushed, you shoved. You laughed, you grinned, you elbowed your way from second through the howling mob pouring onto the field. They reached to touch you, they grabbed at your uniform, your cap was gone, they stabbed at your sweaty hand, they slapped you on the back, on the shoulder, they poked at you, they tapped you on the chest with rolled programs and newspapers, shrieking all the while in furious delight. Dodger fans. It was dusk and from the lower stands they swept upon

the diamond, showering it with a storm of cush-
ions. Panting, exhausted, alone in an ocean of
frenzied fanatics, the Kid finally fought his way
to the players' entrance.

Clack . . . clack . . . clack-clack, clack . . .
clack . . . Up the concrete ramp and into the
dressing room, so filled with players, officials,
men with microphones, photographers, and
reporters one could hardly move. Chisel at the
door tried helplessly to stem the wave of intrud-
ers, to bar entrance to some of the mob. The old
man was beaten back, his arm pushed away.

Inside over the noise and confusion someone
let out a hog call. Roy paused a moment at the
door of Dave's little dressing room. Fans and
players were clapping him on the back and trying to shake his hand but he paid no attention.
Instead he stood watching the old catcher
slumped in a chair while the Doc ripped yards of
tape from his weary body. They were laughing
with him, and someone in the din said something about next year and the next Series.

"Don't make me laugh. Ahh . . . careful
there, Doc, that hurts . . . no, sir, this is the
end, this is. Give it back to the Indians. I've
caught my last game of ball."

"Yeah." Charlie Draper came in hauling the

leather ball bag. "And no one ever caught a better one. Hey, Mac?"

MacManus was at Roy's side in the door, watching Dave in his chair, those yards of tape still being torn off his thighs and legs. "Right, Charlie. What a game he caught. Boy, you could kiss a sweetheart like that."

The Kid's heart jumped. There's the pay-off. That could only mean one thing. Dave was to be manager for next season. Roy seized MacManus by the arm to attract his attention through the uproar.

"Then it's Dave, Mister Mac; now you'll sign him up for next year, won't you?"

The owner turned and looked hard. "Sign him hell! I signed him ten days ago. Before the Series started. Take the pressure off him, to make him loose, see; able to concentrate on running the team." Someone distracted his attention on the other side. "Hullo, Judge . . . thanks . . . thanks lots; but don't congratulate me . . . congratulate Dave and the team. Here . . . meet Roy Tucker, our right fielder, who did as much as anyone to win that game today. Shake hands with Judge Landis, Roy."

The Kid was looking at a white-haired, elderly man with a prominent jaw. MacManus went right

on talking through the confusion, one hand tapping at the Judge's chest, his face close up to
that chin so he could make himself heard.

". . . an' I said before the Series an' I say
right now . . . wouldn't trade him for any right
fielder in the big leagues . . . nosir . . . not for
Masters or Benny Rogers or Pike even . . . you
can have 'em . . . the whole . . . lot. . . ."